"So are you tired of fighting it, Sage?" Ian asked, shifting to face her until his knee was touching her thigh.

"Fighting what?"

"Your attraction to me," Ian said with a grin.

"Ian, you and I can't have a relationship."

"Who said anything about a relationship?"

Why should she be surprised by that? He was Ian Lawrence after all.

"I want you and you want me. It's as simple as that."

"Sex is never that simple," Sage said as she moved closer to the window.

"No, but it can be extremely enjoyable." Ian moved in closer until Sage's back brushed up against the window.

Her eyes fluttered and she knew what was coming next. Ian was so close that she could feel the heat from his thighs and her breasts began to ache with need.

His large hand curled around her neck and he drew her face to his. "You have a deliciously provocative mouth and one that I think can give us both immense pleasure," Ian said, seconds before his mouth covered hers.

Books by Yahrah St. John

Kimani Romance

Never Say Never
Risky Business of Love
Playing for Keeps
This Time for Real
If You So Desire

Kimani Press Arabesque

One Magic Moment
Dare to Love

YAHRAH ST. JOHN

lives in sunny Orlando, but was born in the Windy City, Chicago. A graduate of Hyde Park Career Academy, she earned a bachelor of arts degree in English from Northwestern University.

St. John began writing at the age of twelve and has since written more than twenty short stories and published seven novels. Her books have garnered four-star ratings from *RT Book Reviews*, Rawsistaz Reviewers, Romance in Color and numerous book clubs. A member of Romance Writers of America, St. John is an avid reader of all genres. She enjoys the arts, cooking, traveling, basketball and adventure sports, but her true passion remains writing.

If You So Desire

YAHRAH ST. JOHN

KIMANI
ROMANCE

This book is dedicated to my best friends:
Dimitra Astwood, Therolyn Rodgers, Tiffany Griffin
and Tonya Mitchell, for showing me who my true friends
are and the meaning of sisterhood.

A huge debt of gratitude also goes to my family, friends
and loyal readers for their continued support.

KIMANI PRESS™

ISBN-13: 978-0-373-86178-1

Recycling programs
for this product may
not exist in your area.

IF YOU SO DESIRE

www.kimanipress.com

Printed in U.S.A.

Dear Reader,

I am thrilled to finally have *If You So Desire* hitting the bookshelves. This is Sage Anderson's exciting story and the third book in the Orphan series.

Beautiful and feisty attorney Sage Anderson meets her match when she encounters sexy media mogul Ian Lawrence. Experience the fireworks between this passionate pair as they battle revenge plots and ex-girlfriends while confronting their past fears and insecurities.

And while you're enjoying Sage's story, you'll also get to catch up with some old faves: Quentin, Avery, Malik and Peyton.

Stay tuned for the final tale in the Orphan series in January 2011, in which Chef Dante Moore finds true love with food reviewer Adrianna Wright.

As always, I love hearing from readers and fans, so please feel free to drop me a note at yahrah@yahrahstjohn.com. Also be sure to visit my website at www.yahrahstjohn.com for the latest updates, contests and book signings in your area. Or become a fan on Facebook, LinkedIn, twitter.com/yahrahstjohn or myspace.com/yahrahstjohn.

Warm wishes,

Yahrah St. John

Chapter 1

"I heard through the grapevine that Ian Lawrence is in desperate need of a good labor attorney," Elliott Greenberg, senior partner at Greenberg, Hanson, Waggoner and Associates said during the Monday morning staff meeting. "A former executive has lodged an unprecedented ten-million-dollar lawsuit against him for racial discrimination including lost wages and pain and suffering. His current corporate counsel couldn't get the case settled, so he's looking for a new labor firm."

Ian Lawrence was a wealthy entrepreneur with a multi-media empire that included holdings in publishing, radio and television. His father, Myles Lawrence, was rich and since his death eight years ago, Ian had more than tripled his father's wealth by taking the company public.

"Who's he hired?" Sage inquired.

"Lawrence has scheduled meetings with several high-profile law firms over the next few days, but we're not on the list."

"What do you suggest we do?" partner Dale Hanson replied.

"Someone has to pitch our firm," Elliott returned. "Today."

"Yes, but without an appointment?" Dale asked. "We're a long-shot. If we come in with guns blazing, we'll be shot down."

"In business, Lawrence has always been in favor of the underdog," Peter Waggoner spoke up. "If only to prove everyone wrong when he turns it into a success. We might be a viable alternative, but the right person has to approach him."

"I can do it!" Sage Anderson volunteered from across the table.

Several curious sets of eyes landed on her, a thirty-one-year-old labor associate who'd been with the firm for six years. Her closest friend, Marissa Rodriguez, a family law associate, pinched her arm, but Sage shook her off. She'd already won her last five cases and this could be her big break.

"Sage? *You* want to pitch our firm to Ian Lawrence?" Peter asked.

"Yes, I do. If he's for the underdog as you say—" Sage focused her large almond-shaped eyes on the three gentlemen "—then you can send me, little ol' David, against the big corporate Goliaths."

It wasn't as if she couldn't handle Ian Lawrence. She'd been through worse—growing up at an orphanage with her three longtime friends and family: Quentin Davis, Malik Williams and Dante Moore. When she was eight years old she'd been taken away from her mother, Karen, a known drug addict. Sage had learned at an early age how to deal with men.

Peter rubbed his chin. Sage Anderson was a real spitfire. She was their best labor attorney and annihilated her opponents in the courtroom. Also, the petite woman was a looker and Ian Lawrence was known to be a ladies' man. Her pixie-cut hairdo, beautiful face and figure were sure to attract him. "Do you really think you can convince Lawrence that Greenberg, Hanson, Waggoner and Associates is the law firm for him?"

Sage nodded. "Yes, I can."

"All right, Anderson. You're on, but you'll have your hands full. One of Lawrence's top executives is suing because of racial slurs and because he was demoted when sent to a lesser office and his job given to his Caucasian counterpart."

"Let's hope you can give him that extra push." Elliott slid a piece of paper Sage's way. "He's staying at the Four Seasons."

"But we'll need to prep you first," Peter Waggoner replied, glancing across the table at Sage. "So meeting is adjourned." Once everyone had exited, Elliott and Peter proceeded to prep Sage for the next twenty minutes for her meeting with Ian Lawrence.

"Thank you for the opportunity, Mr. Greenberg," Sage replied, when they had wrapped up the session. She shook his hand. As they walked to the door, Elliott stopped and turned to Sage. "You know you have a lot riding on this."

"I know." *Boy, did she.* Now she just had to convince Ian Lawrence that she was the best lawyer for the job.

Sage returned to her office to mull over the presentation she was about to make. She was jotting down some notes when Marissa knocked on her door.

Marissa was similar to Sage in that she downplayed her

voluptuous Latina features by dressing conservatively in a two-piece pants suit. Unfortunately, she couldn't hide that she was a knockout despite the fact that her long, black hair was rolled in a French roll and her face displayed minimal makeup.

Sage motioned her forward. "Come on in."

"I can't believe they are going to let you pitch to Ian Lawrence without a senior partner present." She and Marissa were both associates and on the partner track.

"Isn't it crazy?" Sage's eyes grew wide with excitement.

"I'm floored." Marissa shook her head in disbelief as she sat down in the chair opposite Sage. "It's unheard-of for an associate to pitch services to a major client."

"I think they are hoping my modest approach works. You know, less is more," Sage replied. "Every other law firm is going to come at Lawrence and show him how big they are. I will pitch to Mr. Lawrence that not only are we a well-respected midsize firm, but he'll get the personal, one-on-one attention that would be missing with all the other firms. The thing is, I have to pitch today. Apparently, he has meetings tomorrow, so I have to talk my way into seeing him."

"Can you do that so quickly?"

"Yes," Sage stated emphatically. She was used to getting the outcome she wanted in the courtroom; Ian Lawrence would be no different.

"The presidential suite at the Four Seasons is ready for you," Jeffrey Smith told his boss, Ian Lawrence, on the ride from the airport to the hotel as he turned off his BlackBerry. As Ian's right-hand business advisor and long-time friend, Jeffrey handled all of his travel arrangements. "Unfortunately, it's not the penthouse, but it has a view of the city and Central Park. Staying at the hotel will give the contractor more time to finish your renovations."

Ian sighed. "I suppose that will have to do." He should have never listened to his ex-girlfriend Lisa Randall and renovated his home.

Jeffrey wasn't fazed by Ian's tone; he was used to his mood swings. "I've scheduled interviews with several prestigious Manhattan law firms that have the finest labor attorneys out there. We'll get this case handled."

"I don't want it handled," Ian replied tersely. "I want it squashed." He'd been served with lawsuit papers in the middle of an important business lunch about acquiring several radio stations in the Midwest. Ian had been utterly embarrassed. "How dare Lucas say he didn't get that promotion because he's not white? I sent him to L.A. a year ago because that's where I needed him. As a black man, I would never discriminate against my own race. Lawrence Enterprises has one of the highest percentages of African-Americans in high-profile positions in the country. Anyone who knows me knows that Lucas's accusation is completely ludicrous."

"And we'll disprove it or settle if we have to."

"After everything my father did for him, there's no way I'm going to give that man one red cent of my money. I will not settle." Ian folded his arms across his chest.

Jeffrey glanced at his best friend. Why did Ian have to be so stubborn? "Do you really want to have this case tried out in the media and in the court of public opinion? Because trust me, that's what it's going to come to."

"Of course not." Ian turned sharply and glared at Jeffrey. "But I won't have Lucas run roughshod over me. I would not have gotten where I am today if I let someone get away with that."

When he'd taken over as CEO of Lawrence Enterprises

when his father had passed away eight years ago, the board had been wary of him. He was a thirty-year-old upstart. They'd all thought they understood what the vision of the company should be better than he, but Ian had other plans. He'd shown each and every one of them that he was a force to be reckoned with.

"So this is about your ego? Instead of what's right for the company?" Jeffrey inquired. "You know some members of the board would love for you to falter, especially Bruce Hoffman. He didn't take it too kindly when you squashed the television station acquisition deal that he'd worked on for months."

Ian couldn't care less about Bruce Hoffman. Bruce was behind the racist remarks that fueled Lucas's lawsuit, but Ian had a feeling it went much deeper. Was this Lucas's payback for what he perceived happened with Gia Smith all those years ago? He'd thought they'd put it behind them, but maybe he was wrong.

When the limo stopped, Ian quickly exited the vehicle. He didn't wait for Jeffrey; instead, he walked through the door held open by one of the doormen and headed for the elevators.

Jeffrey smiled as he entered the lobby and took care of the details with the hotel clerk. He had offended Ian, but he'd get over it. He was probably the only person Ian allowed to give it to him straight. That bluntness was why Ian respected him and why their twenty-year friendship had endured Ian's father's death and Jeffrey's failed marriage.

When Jeffrey obtained the key cards from the clerk, he joined Ian by the elevators. At six feet three, Ian was taller than Jeffrey's six feet, but Jeffrey was not intimidated. The elevator swished open seconds later and the two men entered the cab.

"It's not about my ego," Ian answered once the doors shut.

"No?"

"No," Ian stated firmly and turned his dark eyes on Jeffrey. "Settling with that bastard will make me appear guilty, which I'm not."

"Settling might save the company money in the long run and not tarnish your image."

"Like it isn't already tarnished." Ian chuckled to himself. He read the tabloids and knew he was viewed as a jet-setting playboy with a huge conglomerate as his toy. He had money. Cars. Clothes. And of course, women. Lots of women.

His name had been linked with several models and starlets and, sure, they'd amused him for the short time he'd spent in their company, but none had held his interest for long. Women couldn't be trusted. He'd learned that for himself when his own mother ran away with her lover and left her eight-year-old son to be raised by nannies. Fate, however, had not been on her side and she and her lover had been killed in a car crash in Rome the following year.

"True," Jeffrey agreed. "And you play into it every time."

"I do not," Ian said as they exited the elevator. "Matter of fact, I'm done with women." His last dalliance had severely soured him against the opposite sex. Lisa Randall, a leggy model, had started hearing wedding bells after casually dating for six months. When he'd told her it wasn't going to happen, she'd kicked him to the curb and high-tailed it on a plane to Paris.

"Sure you are." Jeffrey opened the doors to the presidential suite.

"I am," Ian replied, storming through them. "All I want to do now is relax and take a hot shower." He flopped down on the sofa, unbuttoned his suit jacket and loosened his tie. "Can you schedule a massage for me?"

"No problem," Jeffrey replied. "I'm going to my room to attend to a few details for tomorrow's meetings."

"You know there is more than enough room in this suite for you," Ian replied. The two-bedroom suite had separate marble bathrooms as well as a living room, butler's pantry and its own private terrace.

"Yes, but I like my privacy." Although he and Ian got along tremendously, they spent a great deal of time in each other's company.

"Carry on, then." Ian waved him off and closed his eyes. Kicking off his shoes, he took a short nap. After the early morning flight from LAX, he was exhausted. He awoke nearly an hour later and retired to the bathroom for a much-needed hot shower.

In the lobby of the Four Seasons, Sage looked over her notes as she sat on the plush leather sofa. Mr. Waggoner and Mr. Greenberg had given her some suggestions on what to say and she'd brought the representation agreement. Now she just had to convince Ian Lawrence to sign it.

Sage sighed. She'd volunteered because she was the best labor attorney in the firm and they knew it. She'd won all of her last five cases and had a solid record, but was that enough against the corporate mammoths? She would find out. Closing her briefcase, Sage rose and headed for the elevator, but stopped mid-step for a pit stop to the restroom for a final check of her appearance. Once inside, she set her briefcase on the floor and reached for the compact inside her purse.

Today was a good day. While waiting in the lobby, she'd overheard the concierge making dinner arrangements for Ian and discovered he was staying in the presidential suite.

Sage glanced at her reflection in the mirror and was pleased with what she saw. She looked professional in her pin-striped suit, white V-neck collar shirt and peep-toe black pumps. Her short hairdo was stylishly cut and after a little powder to her nose and a glide of lipstick to refresh her lips, she was all set. She looked like a competent lawyer and one well worthy to take on the dashing media mogul.

She exited the restroom and caught the private elevator just as the doors closed.

"Ma'am, this elevator is reserved for special guests," the occupant said.

"I know," Sage returned smoothly. "I am Mr. Lawrence's attorney."

The Asian woman smiled back at her. "I am his masseuse."

Ian Lawrence was stressed, was he? Well, Sage had the cure for what ailed him. When the private elevator stopped on the fifty-first floor, Sage headed to suite 5101 while the masseuse went to suite 5102. Clearly, the woman had been given the wrong room number, but Sage wasn't going to mention it. She needed the extra time to get her foot in the door.

She found the door slightly ajar when she arrived. Sage knocked several times and when no one answered, she cautiously entered. "Hello?" she called out again. Her footsteps echoed on the immaculate marble floor. As she glanced around, Sage couldn't help but be impressed with the living room decor. The yellow and gold overtones and pearlized metallic cabinets gave it a sumptuous feel. Oil paintings and a plasma television adorned the walls, but the true feature was the baby grand piano. *Was this how the rich and famous lived?*

She was admiring the spectacular view of Central Park from the floor-to-ceiling window when she felt someone's presence behind her. She spun around on her heel and found Ian Lawrence standing in the buff drying himself off with a towel which barely covered that intimate part of him. Sage couldn't help but stare and take in every chiseled inch of his six-foot-three frame from his smooth peanut butter complexion to his sensuously full lips and goatee to his well-toned abs and muscular thighs.

"Ohmigod!" Embarrassed, Sage turned away. She had no idea how breathtakingly splendid he'd be in person. It didn't help that he was standing behind her without a stitch of clothing on.

Ian smiled broadly before wrapping the towel around his mid-section. "I'm sure I'm not the first man you've seen naked."

"Excuse me?" Sage whirled around.

"You are the masseuse. Are you not?" Ian asked, responding to her haughty expression. "Some people do like to get massaged in their birthday suits."

"Do I look like a masseuse?" Sage gestured to her clothing.

Ian's brow furrowed together. She didn't look like a masseuse. Of course he hadn't really been looking at her attire. He'd been fixated on her beautiful face, which was always his downfall. He loved beautiful things. "Well, if you're not my masseuse, who the hell are you?"

"I'm— I'm— I'm Sage Anderson." Sage walked toward Ian with her hand extended when all of sudden, she felt her chest tighten. Her purse and briefcase dropped with a loud thud to the floor. The all-too-familiar feeling of anxiety and panic overtook her and Sage began wheezing uncontrollably.

"Are you okay?" Ian rushed toward her.

Sage gasped several times trying to catch her breath. "I'll…I'll be okay, just give me a minute." She reached for the couch, but couldn't make it. Ian grabbed her hand and assisted her to the sofa.

"What can I do?" he asked. Her face had drained of color and she was beginning to sweat. For the first time in a long time, Ian felt utterly helpless.

Sage clutched her chest as her breathing became more rapid. *Why did this have to happen to her now?* "My inhaler…"

"Where is it?"

"Purse," Sage managed to eke out.

Ian rummaged through her purse until he found an asthma inhaler. He quickly brought the inhaler to Sage's lips and she clutched his muscular arm as she sucked in the medication.

After several moments passed, Sage slowly released Ian's arm and lay back against the sofa. Ian breathed a huge sigh of relief when her coloring returned and she began to breathe normally.

"Thank you," Sage said. She was so embarrassed. She hadn't had an asthma attack in a long time. Had the sight of Ian Lawrence's naked body brought it on? She'd have thought other body parts would have reacted to his virile male presence.

"No problem," Ian said, looking down at her. "Just relax." He leaned over and brushed several tendrils of hair out of her face. Sage Anderson was really quite stunning. She had more natural beauty than any of the models he'd encountered.

Sage was surprised by Ian's simple act of kindness. She wouldn't have suspected that he would be the gentle-giant type. If she let herself, she could get lost in those cobalt eyes and amazingly long lashes, but she couldn't. She'd come here to convince Ian Lawrence to give her firm his case. She had to regroup and not lose sight of her objective no matter how intensely he was staring at her.

Once her breathing calmed and she was on an even keel, Ian asked. "So why don't you tell me why you're really here, Sage?"

She didn't like that he'd so casually used her first name, but what could she do? He'd already gotten her out of a pickle.

"I came to pitch my law firm, Greenberg, Hanson, Waggoner and Associates," Sage answered, straightening her back.

"My assistant Jeffrey handles all of my appointments."

"I'm sure he does." Sage found the strength to rise from the sofa. "But I didn't have an appointment."

"Ah, there's the rub." Ian smiled and revealed a set of even white teeth. He watched as she carefully walked over to her briefcase that was lying in the middle of the living-room floor before turning around to face him. She was petite with just the right amount of curves. He enjoyed picking up his women and carrying them off to bed.

"Aren't you going to get dressed now?" Sage inquired.

"Why?" Ian peered at her. "If you're going to ambush me in my hotel room—" he folded his arms across his broad chest and settled back into the sofa "—you should be prepared for the unexpected."

"You want me to give a presentation with you wearing nothing more than a towel?"

Ian nodded.

Just then, a knock sounded at the front door. "Would you mind?" Ian asked Sage.

Did she look like his servant? Instead of expressing her thoughts aloud, she walked to the door and opened it. It was the masseuse. She followed Sage to the living room with her massage bed tucked underneath her arm.

"Would you mind giving us a few minutes?" Ian asked the masseuse. He was having such a great time watching Sage squirm, he didn't want their encounter to end. "If it's not too much trouble, I'd love a cup of tea. I believe there's some in the butler's pantry."

"No problem, Mr. Lawrence." The masseuse sat the table down and bowed before leaving the room.

"Do continue." Ian waved his hand.

Sage glared at him before saying, "My law firm can get this lawsuit dropped before it even goes to court."

"Other law firms will be telling me the same thing tomorrow morning," he replied. "What makes you any different?"

"Greenberg, Hanson, Waggoner and Associates are not as large as some of those firms," Sage returned. "Which means you'll get more one-on-one interaction with your attorney and the senior partners."

"Oh." Ian's brow rose slightly. "One-on-one interaction is exactly what I like, especially if it's coming from you."

Sage colored and was about to respond to his overt flirtation when the door to the suite opened and an attractive gentleman walked into the living room. Although he wasn't nearly as tall or as built as Ian, he wasn't bad to look at either.

Jeffrey glanced first at the beautiful woman in the suit and then at Ian, who looked rather comfortable considering he was bare-chested with a towel wrapped around his middle. "Ian, what's going on?"

"Ms. Anderson, here—" Ian nodded to Sage "—was just pitching her law firm to me, a Greenberg…" His voice trailed off as his eyes made contact with her large expressive brown ones.

"Hanson, Waggoner and Associates," Sage finished. She rose to her feet. "You must be Jeffrey Smith."

"I am," Jeffrey said. "And if you know who I am, then you also know that we did not have an appointment."

Ian watched their interchange and saw a sheepish smile spread across Sage's face. "I realize that, Mr. Smith, but my firm—" Sage handed him a folder "—is more than capable of representing Mr. Lawrence in this suit and I would love to discuss the opportunity in further detail, once Mr. Lawrence is properly attired, of course."

Jeffrey glanced at Ian. "Do you intend on changing, Ian, or are you going to sit there in the buff all day?"

"I was waiting," Ian began, "for my masseuse. And here she is." He nodded to the Asian woman who'd returned from the pantry with a tea set on a tray. "Now, if you'll both excuse me, I'm going to finally have that massage. Ms. Anderson, Jeffrey." Ian nodded before retiring to the spare bedroom with the masseuse.

Once he'd gone, Sage returned her attention back to the subject at hand. "I know our introduction was somewhat unorthodox," Sage said, "but when I found the suite door open, I walked inside. I really had no idea I'd find Mr. Lawrence indisposed. My business card, Mr. Smith, is inside the folder and has all the particulars. Please do give me a call. We'd love the opportunity to represent you."

"Thank you, Ms. Anderson, for your time." Jeffrey shook her hand. The woman sure had chutzpah showing up at Ian's suite unannounced.

Sage grabbed her briefcase and purse and headed out of the door. Once she made it inside the private elevator, she kicked the interior cab wall. She'd screwed that up royally. *What was she going to tell the senior partners?*

After Ian's hour-long massage, he returned to the living room and found Jeffrey working on his laptop at the desk.

Jeffrey glanced up. "You're clothed now," he commented. Ian was dressed in pressed slacks and a button-down shirt.

Ian grinned mischievously. "About earlier." He walked over to the bar, screwed open a bottle of water and sipped liberally. "It was obvious Sage Anderson was completely caught off guard at finding me half-naked. So I thought I'd have a little fun with her."

Jeffrey glanced over the top of his glasses. "It didn't look like that to me."

"What do you mean?" Ian asked, sitting on the sofa.

"C'mon, Ian." Jeffrey closed the lid of his laptop. "I've known you long enough to know when you're interested in a woman."

"All right, you caught me." He grinned. He'd found the uptight lawyer not only beautiful but sexy as hell. "She was hot, wasn't she?"

"I really wasn't looking."

"How could you not?" Ian inquired, annoyed at Jeffrey's aloofness. "Anyway, I want you to investigate her and get back to me by tomorrow afternoon." He was curious about Sage Anderson and wanted to know what made her tick.

"You sure don't want much," Jeffrey replied. It amazed him how Ian snapped his fingers and just expected him to make miracles happen.

Ian ignored Jeffrey's tone. "Just get it to me by tomorrow." If Sage Anderson's law firm was any good, perhaps he wouldn't have to go through all those endless interviews over the next couple of days. Maybe he'd already found the right one.

Chapter 2

"I'm in such hot water," Sage announced when she walked into her friend Dante Moore's tapas bar that evening. The rest of their quasi family, Quentin Davis, his fiancée Avery Roberts, Malik Williams and his girlfriend Peyton Sawyer, were already assembled.

"Why? What happened?" Quentin asked when she walked over and joined them at the bar for a cocktail.

Without her having to ask, Dante slid over Sage's favorite drink, an apple martini, from behind the bar.

Sage threw down her briefcase on the counter. "Thank you, I needed this." She took a generous sip. "I volunteered to pitch our firm to multimedia mogul Ian Lawrence."

"I've heard of him," Malik replied, rubbing his permanent five-o'clock shadow. "He has one of the most successful black media enterprises around. Is he in some kind of trouble?"

"I can't get into it. All I can say is, he's looking at several law firms in Manhattan, but ours wasn't one of them."

"Is that why you're in hot water?" Quentin asked. He'd always had a soft spot for Sage. She was like his baby sister and he didn't like seeing her so distressed. He had been preoccupied of late with his and Avery's wedding plans and a photo spread he was shooting for *Vibe* magazine and they hadn't spent enough time together.

Sage hung her head low. "No. I volunteered to pitch our firm to Lawrence and it was a bust. How am I going to show my face tomorrow?" She shook her head in disgust. When she'd finally made it back to the office to work on her other cases, the senior partners had thankfully left early for a golf game leaving her blissfully in peace, at least for now. Once they found out what a royal mess she'd made out of her pitch, they might send her packing.

"Why don't you take it from the top?" Malik asked, turning toward her. Sage was known to be somewhat of a drama queen. Even when they were little, she'd made a mountain out of a mole hill. The only person who fell for it every time was Quentin.

Sage rolled her eyes at Malik. "Well, I didn't have an appointment, so I snuck in his suite only to find him naked in his living room. That's when out of nowhere I had an asthma attack."

Quentin frowned. Sage rarely had attacks anymore unless she was really stressed. "Are you okay?" He grabbed her by the shoulder and stared at her intently.

"Well, are you?" Dante replied, when she didn't answer right away.

Sage nodded and pulled away. "Yes, I'm fine. I guess I just panicked for a minute. Although Ian Lawrence was kind enough to get my inhaler, he made me pitch our firm to him while he sat there wearing nothing but a towel. It was completely embarrassing."

"If he likes being in the buff, maybe he'd be interested in posing for my art class," Avery spoke for the first time. Because of her expertise as an art buyer for the Henri Lawrence Gallery in Soho, Malik had asked her to teach an art class at the Harlem Community Center he oversaw.

Sage glared at Avery, but everyone else chuckled.

"Were you embarrassed by the fact that you flubbed the pitch or by the fact that you were attracted to him?" Dante inquired. He hadn't seen that interested glint in Sage's eye since she was with her ex James Wilson in law school.

"I wasn't attracted to him," Sage huffed. She hated that Dante could read her so well.

"No?" Quentin asked and peered into her almond-shaped eyes. "Are you sure about that? I can't even recall the last time you had an asthma attack."

"Yeah," Malik asked, getting in on the razzing. "When was the last time you were out on a date, Sage?"

"All right, boys." Peyton jumped in to stop them from ganging up on Sage. "Let the woman speak."

"What does that have to do with anything?" Sage asked. "I work seventy-hour workweeks. Where am I going to find men like you guys in New York anyway?" Dante, Quentin and Malik were not only her family, but good, honest, upstanding men. Plus, they were absolutely gorgeous. Quentin with his Hershey-chocolate good looks and bald head, Malik with his dreads, toffee complexion and five-o'clock shadow and Dante with his clean-cut caramel self and sexy goatee were all fine.

"You have to make yourself available." Malik came around the bar and wrapped his arms around Sage's shoulders. "You can't be all work all the time. You have to live a little."

"Look who's talking." Sage could remember a time when Malik was all work and no play. The community centers he oversaw had been Malik's whole life. That was until he met Peyton, a professor at NYU, last year. "Besides, I am interested in Ian Lawrence in a professional capacity only," Sage responded.

"Sure you are, Sage," Dante replied. "Sure you are."

"How'd it go?" Marissa asked, barging into her office the next morning.

"I flubbed my presentation."

Marissa's nose crinkled into a frown. It was unlike Sage to tank anything. She was a true perfectionist and knew labor law like the back of her hand. "Why? Did something happen?"

"Yes, something happened," Sage said, rising from her chair and closing her office door. "I found Ian Lawrence stark-naked in his room." Sage leaned against the door.

"You didn't." Marissa gasped and covered her mouth with her hand.

"I did. And he made me give my presentation while he wore a towel and a smile." She'd left that part out when she discussed the meeting with Peter before Marissa arrived.

"That had to be quite a sight," Marissa replied. "From the pictures, the man is fine."

"Even more so in person." Sage pushed away from the door and paced the floor. "And I might have gotten through to him if his assistant hadn't come in and ushered me out."

"Perhaps it's not as bad you think," Marissa said. "He has a lot of firms to meet. We could still be in the running."

"I doubt very seriously that Ian Lawrence will give me or the firm a second thought," Sage replied.

* * *

Interviews with the prestigious law firms Jeffrey had set up were held in one of the conference rooms of the Four Seasons. Ian and Jeffrey listened for two days as each firm expounded on their achievements and yet Ian wasn't ready to make a decision. He was happy when lunch drew near and they could adjourn the interview process.

"Have you found anything on Sage Anderson yet?" Ian asked as he and Jeffrey entered 57, one of Four Seasons' restaurants. He was anxious to find out more about the attractive lawyer.

"No, not yet," Jeffrey replied when the hostess seated them. "Mark should have something shortly." He kept the shrewd private investigator on retainer whenever he needed a dossier on someone or information of a delicate nature.

"Well, tell him it's of the utmost importance," Ian replied. "I want to know everything about her before the day is out."

"What's your rush?" Jeffrey replied, accepting the menu from the maître d'.

"I'm just curious."

Jeffrey doubted that was the real reason but remained mum. When his BlackBerry vibrated in his pocket, he answered. "Hello. Okay, thank you for the heads-up."

Ian looked at Jeffrey. "What's going on?"

"You have bigger fish to fry, my friend." He'd just been informed that Ian's ex-girlfriend Lisa Randall had arrived at the Four Seasons and demanded to be taken up to his suite. The hotel clerk had called Jeffrey to give him a heads-up. Ian was not going to be pleased. "Lisa's in your suite."

"What?" Ian's voice rose. "What the hell is she doing here? And how did she know where I was?"

Jeffrey shrugged. "You would know better than I."

"How would I know?" Ian replied. "I haven't heard a word from her in two months."

"Well, she's here now."

Ian sucked his teeth. He was in no mood for romantic entanglements. When she'd stormed out of his apartment, he'd been relieved. He could continue his playboy ways—and now Sage Anderson was on his radar. He was hoping for a quick romp around in the sheets with the beautiful attorney, but Lisa's presence could ruin his plans.

"I'll handle her," Ian replied. "Once and for all."

Ian found Lisa in his suite unpacking her Louis Vuitton luggage.

"Lisa!" He called out her name.

Startled, she spun around to face him. Despite how angry he was with her, Ian couldn't deny she was still a beautiful specimen. She had a long mass of wavy black hair, some of which was hers, milk-chocolate skin and legs that went on for miles.

"Ian, darling." Lisa swished across the thick plush carpet and slid her arms beneath his suit jacket. Lisa was nothing like Sage Anderson, who although petite had curves in all the right places while Lisa was slender and nearly matched him in height at five foot eleven.

"I've missed you." When she tried to kiss Ian on the lips, he turned his head.

"Why are you here, Lisa?" Ian inquired. "Things have been over between us for quite some time."

"Are they?" she asked, grabbing Ian's lapel. She focused her tigerlike eyes on his cobalt ones. "As I recall, we had a little tiff. That doesn't mean we're over."

"That's exactly what it means." Ian removed her hands from his lapel and moved away from her embrace. "You left for Paris and I haven't seen or heard a word from you. Now you come back and are unpacking your things—" he nodded to the open suitcases "—as if nothing has happened. Well, I'm here to tell you that this ship has sailed, baby. We're over."

"No, no, no." Lisa furiously shook her head and her hair went flying in every direction. "I refuse to believe that after six months together that things will end this way between us."

"You knew the score," Ian replied. "I never lied to you." He'd thought things between them were great. She was a perfect companion when they were jet-setting off to parts unknown or going to a movie premiere or being photographed by the paparazzi, and she was great in bed. But it was in between, during those quiet moments, that had caused Lisa to want more than Ian was ready to give.

"C'mon, we're good together." Lisa slinked next to Ian and rubbed her small breasts against his chest. "Can't I convince you to give me a second chance? I know I can get you out of this bad mood." She reached down for the buckle on his pants, but he flung her hand away.

"I said no, Lisa." Why was she forcing him to treat her with contempt? Why couldn't she leave with a little grace and dignity?

"Well, that's a switch," Lisa said scathingly and stormed to the bureau and starting throwing items back into her suitcase. When she was finished, she slammed her suitcase shut.

Ian scratched his head. She was right. He never turned down sex until today. "I guess it is."

"You don't know what you're missing, Ian Lawrence."

"Oh, I think I do." Drama. Drama. And more drama.

Lisa flung her purse over her shoulder and gave him a withering look. "Just you wait. You'll be begging to have me back in no time." It was rare that a man like Ian was available and she wasn't going to give up without a fight.

She would just have to bide her time and strike when the iron was hot.

"I highly doubt that, Lisa," Ian returned.

Seconds later, the door slammed shut. Ian breathed a huge sigh of relief and fell back on the king-size bed. He glanced up when he saw an American flag being waved from the doorway a short while later.

"Is it safe to enter?" Jeffrey poked his head around the corner.

"Yes, it is." Ian waved him in.

"Good." Jeffrey came forward. "Because I have the report on Sage Anderson."

He tried to hand Ian the folder, but Ian shook his head. Lisa had given him a headache and he was no mood to read a long dosier. "Why don't you give me the skinny?"

"No problem." Jeffrey opened the folder. "Sage Anderson was placed in foster care at age eight because her mother was a drug addict. She wasn't adopted because of her constant sickliness and was sent to live in an orphanage."

"It sounds like she had a rough childhood. Does it say what the sickness was?"

"It was as simple as asthma," Jeffrey replied. "But at the time the families in foster care were so poor that she was never diagnosed until she went to the orphanage."

Ian was intrigued. "So how does a poor, asthmatic orphan end up as a successful labor attorney?"

"It's a classic story of a woman pulling herself up by her bootstraps," Jeffrey replied. "She was valedictorian at her high school, graduated summa cum laude at NYU and went to NYU's law school where she was second in her class only to her ex-fiancé, a James Wilson."

"I'm amazed at what she accomplished given all the obstacles she had to endure." Ian rubbed his jaw. "Wait, did you say fiancé?"

"I did, but he's an ex." Jeffrey nodded. "Apparently the pair broke off their engagement shortly after law school. The report goes on to say that she along with several of her friends, all men, by the way." He threw that in for good measure, better Ian know that he could have some competition. "They grew up together in the same orphanage. They roomed together when they were struggling in their early twenties, but now they're all successful. One's a well-known photographer, Quentin Davis. I think you have some of his work. Another is Dante Moore, a local restaurateur. The third is Malik Williams, a director of several community centers for Children's Aid Network."

Ian rose from the bed and went over to look out the window. He admired her fortitude and resilience. Life had thrown her lemons, but she had made lemonade. Sage Anderson was just the kind of woman and lawyer he was looking for.

"Cancel the rest of the appointments." Ian turned around and told Jeffrey. "We've found our attorney."

Sage nervously wrung her hands in her office. It was Wednesday afternoon and the senior partners had not yet approached her about the results of her meeting with Ian due to an unexpected snafu on a class-action lawsuit. Sage prepared herself for the inevitable, to be fired. She wasn't sure what she would do after this, but somehow she would pull through. She hadn't gotten where she was today by giving up. She nearly jumped out of her skin when her assistant buzzed her phone. "Hello?"

"You have a visitor, Ms. Anderson."

Sage paused, took a deep breath and said, "Send him in."

Sage closed her eyes when the door opened and took a deep breath. When she opened them, she found Ian

Lawrence standing in her office. His tall, overpowering presence filled her doorway.

"Ms. Anderson." Ian came toward her desk and offered his hand.

Sage stared down at his large masculine hand and blinked several times to make sure she wasn't seeing things.

"Ms. Anderson?" Ian asked. She looked as if she were ready to faint.

"Uh…uh, yes," Sage stammered and shook his hand. "Mr. Lawrence, what are you doing here?" And why did he have to look so darn good? The Italian suit he wore only enhanced his broad shoulders and muscular figure. Sage remembered all too well how his skin had glistened from the shower. How the water pellets had clung to his chiseled chest and thighs. He'd invaded her dreams and she'd gotten little sleep the past two evenings.

Ian watched Sage underneath hooded lashes. She looked just as beautiful as the day she'd barged into his hotel room. Not to mention the fact that she was flushed. Her warm brown complexion could not hide her surprise at his coming in person to her office. That was good. He liked that she was a little off balance. It would make the chase all the more fun.

"I gave your firm's proposal serious review."

"You did?" Sage held her breath.

"Yes. And you intrigue me, Ms. Anderson," Ian replied, walking over to her window and looking down below.

"How so?"

"Not many attorneys would have had the nerve to talk their way into my hotel room without an appointment. I admire your chutzpah." Ian turned and smiled at her.

"As I recall, I didn't do a very good job," Sage replied,

leaning back in her chair. A memory of her clutching his muscular arm came to mind.

"Ah, yes." Ian rubbed his goatee thoughtfully. "Your asthma attack was quite an introduction." Ian moved from the window and was dangerously close to her. He was perched on the edge of her desk as if he owned the place.

"I don't scare easily, Ms. Anderson." Ian stared down at her.

When he did, Sage's heart went pitter-pat. She didn't know if it was his musky cologne or the seductive way he was staring at her, but Ian's nearness was sending her hormones into overdrive. Sage couldn't recall a time when she'd been this unglued around a man. What was it about Ian that caused her to stutter and act like a complete idiot? She'd been up against more intimidating men in the courtroom.

"In fact," Ian continued, straightening his stance, "I came to tell you in person that I have decided to let Greenberg, Hanson, Waggoner and Associates represent me in this matter."

"You have?" a masculine voice said from behind them.

Sage and Ian both turned and found Peter Waggoner standing at the doorway.

"And you are?" Ian asked.

Sage skirted from behind her desk and past Ian's looming presence to Peter. "Mr. Lawrence, this is Peter Waggoner, one of our senior partners."

"Mr. Waggoner." The two gentlemen shook hands.

"This comes as quite a surprise." Peter's brow rose and he gave Sage a bewildered look. "But we are pleased that you would consider our firm. We'll assemble the best team to handle your case."

"So long as that *team* is headed by Ms. Anderson," Ian

returned. He glanced in Sage's direction. "She is the reason I've agreed to allow your firm to represent me."

Sage stood back in awe of Ian. After her pitching debacle, Peter had most certainly come in to give her her walking papers. She loved the way Ian had just put Peter in his place. She liked a man who took charge.

"Of course, of course." Peter smiled.

Ian reached into his suit pocket and pulled out a card. "Here's my assistant's card. Set up an appointment with him and he'll iron out the particulars."

"Right away." Peter shook Ian's hand one final time and left the room.

Sage turned around to face Ian. "Mr. Lawrence, I really appreciate the opportunity." She offered her hand. "I assure you your faith in me and our firm is not misplaced."

"I'm sure it isn't," Ian returned smoothly. But instead of letting her hand go, he lingered for several excruciatingly long moments before releasing it. "I look forward to working with you." And with that comment, Ian Lawrence disappeared just as quickly as he'd come.

After he'd gone, Sage was speechless and plopped down in her chair. What had happened just now? Was she the only one feeling the sexual tension? Or had there been a spark of interest in Ian's eyes, too? No, no, surely she'd imagined it. Or at least she hoped so, otherwise this would be a very complicated situation, indeed.

"I got the case," Sage told Dante when she stopped by his tapas bar that evening.

"Congratulations, Sage." Dante gave her a bear hug. "And here you thought you'd blown it. How about I fix you up something special?"

"That sounds great, Dante." Sage followed him into his stainless-steel kitchen. "This is really going to be a great opportunity for me." She nodded to the sous chef and several other workers getting ready for the dinner rush. "This is exactly the kind of case I need to make partner."

"Do you really think so?" Dante asked, taking a cut-up chicken fryer and potatoes out of the refrigerator, and some oregano, olive oil, capers and white wine out of the cupboard. Sage smiled as she saw the ingredients. Dante was making one of her favorite dishes: chicken vesuvio.

Sage nodded and hopped onto the opposite counter. "You should have seen the look on the senior partner's face when Ian told him in no uncertain terms that I will spearhead his defense or he'd be taking his business elsewhere. It was priceless."

"Sounds like more than just the case got you excited," Dante replied, seasoning the chicken with coarse salt, black pepper and oregano.

"If you're going to start in on me again about Ian Lawrence, then I'll tell you again that you're dead wrong," Sage replied, folding her arms across her chest. "Sure, he's attractive. I don't deny that, but I can't get involved with my client." It would be the worst possible career move she could make getting involved in a sex scandal with Ian Lawrence, no matter how pleasurable it might be.

"All right." Dante threw his hands up in the air and went back to cooking. "I just want to be sure before you get yourself into something you can't get yourself out of."

"Trust me, Dante. I have the situation with Ian Lawrence handled."

"So, you've decided to hire Sage Anderson's law firm," Jeffrey said over a nightcap in Ian's suite later that evening as they sat on the sofa. He'd known that Ian wouldn't be able to resist a pretty face. "It's fortunate that the best labor attorney in the city is also a beautiful woman."

"It won't be a problem." Ian sipped on his scotch.

"How can you be so sure?"

"Because…" He'd seen the same attraction in her that he felt. Sage Anderson wanted him as much as he wanted her.

"Because no woman can resist you?" Jeffrey asked.

"Not every woman, just this woman." Ian grinned. And when the time was right he and Sage would be sharing a bed.

Chapter 3

"It's quite a coup you've achieved, Sage," Peter commented from her office doorway the following morning. The other partners were in disbelief when he'd told them that a female associate had secured one of the biggest profile cases of the year. It had been a long shot, but Sage had pulled it off.

"Thank you, Mr. Waggoner." It was not every day she got kudos from a senior partner.

"No, it is I who should be thanking you." Peter pointed to himself and then to Sage. "Lawrence could have easily overlooked our firm if you hadn't convinced him to allow us to represent him. By the way, how did you charm him?"

"I can't give away my trade secrets now, can I?"

"You have to know that this case is going to secure your making partner this year."

The magic word, thought Sage. *Partner.* After all the long hours and the sacrifices she'd made, after growing up with nothing and being shuttled from foster home to foster home before coming to the orphanage, she deserved this. She'd given up a lot for her career. Her one and only love, James, had cheated on her because he claimed she wasn't there for him anymore.

After law school, she'd been so driven to succeed, to have a career to rely on. Although she wanted to get married one day and have a family, she didn't want to end up destitute and alone like her drug-addicted mother. So she'd clocked in long hours at the firm, causing James to develop a wandering eye. She'd been devastated to find him in their bed with another woman. After their seven-year courtship had come to a bitter end, she'd turned all her focus to the law. If everything went according to plan, she would be the first African-American and the first woman to become partner at Greenberg, Hanson, Waggoner and Associates.

"Yes, I do."

"Then I know you will ensure that we win this lawsuit."

"I will," Sage responded.

After he'd left, a slight bit of self-doubt crept into Sage's mind. What if she didn't win? Was she ready to start at the bottom with a new firm?

"Legal reviewed the representation documents from Greenberg, Hanson, Waggoner and Associates," Jeffrey said while he and Ian ate breakfast on the terrace overlooking Central Park.

"And?" Ian inquired, taking a forkful of his Greek omelet.

"They are in order. Exorbitant fees like most law firms, but nothing out of the ordinary," Jeffrey replied. "All I need is for you to sign them." He slid the documents across the table.

"I don't have anything to write with," Ian replied.

Jeffrey reached inside his suit pocket, produced a pen and handed it to Ian.

"Thank you." Ian scribbled his signature on the documents.

"By the way, Sage Anderson has requested a meeting with you to go over the details of the case."

"Excellent." Ian brought his coffee cup to his lips. "Schedule it over dinner tomorrow night."

"Ian." Jeffrey sighed. "I have to caution you that you are moving into dangerous territory here."

"And when has that ever deterred me?" Ian asked with a smile. He would not have increased the value of Lawrence Enterprises' holdings without taking risks. The company now owned several television and radio stations in addition to the publishing company his father started. Sure, some of the older men on the board had questioned his judgment when he'd taken over as CEO of the company, but they'd soon realized that he was the future when their pocketbooks began getting fatter.

"Lucas Johnson has hired Sullivan and Watkins and they are out for your blood, Ian," Jeffrey responded. "You can't dismiss this as just a frivolous lawsuit. The entire business community will be looking at how this suit plays out. To have an African-American employee suing an African-American owner for discrimination is big news. The company can't afford for your judgment to become clouded because another body part has taken over," Jeffrey said plainly.

"I heard you the first time," Ian replied testily. Despite their long friendship, he didn't appreciate Jeffrey questioning his actions. "Just do as I say and schedule a dinner with Sage at Jean Georges."

"Fine. Consider it done." Jeffrey closed his organizer. He knew when to back off.

"Please schedule to have my Armani suit pressed and ready for me by six-thirty sharp," Ian replied.

"Will do," Jeffrey said, taking his leave.

Ian had no intention of altering his plans, not when he had someone as intriguing as Sage Anderson just within his reach.

Sage nervously put down the receiver. When she'd called Jeffrey, she'd anticipated a business meeting with Ian at her office. Instead, Jeffrey had informed her that Ian was busy for the duration of the afternoon and would only be available for dinner tomorrow.

Dinner was exactly what they didn't need. It was impossible to deny that when they were in the same room there was a spark between them. She'd felt it yesterday afternoon when he'd personally stopped by to inform her he'd like to retain their services. It was something his assistant could have easily taken care of, but instead Ian had taken the time to personally come and hire them.

Sage needed to interview him in order to get started on the case. So she had no choice but to accept his dinner invitation to Jean Georges.

When Friday arrived, she purposely did not go home to change because she wanted to reiterate this dinner was not a date. It was a business meeting. Her pearls, cream-and-black knee-length pleated dress and matching jacket would have to be suitable enough. Ian needed to know that their relationship had boundaries.

When security rang her office to let her know that his car was downstairs, Sage grabbed her briefcase with trepidation. *Breathe, just breathe,* she told herself. She didn't need another asthma attack. He was just a man after all. *One fine-looking man.*

The short elevator ride was interminable as Sage reminded herself to forget the man and remain professional. It was easier said than done when the chauffeur opened the door and she found Ian Lawrence sprawled across the backseat of his Bentley.

"Are you getting in?" he asked when Sage paused at the door.

"Of course." She smiled as the chauffeur helped her inside.

"I'm looking forward to dinner with you." Ian turned to Sage and his eyes roved her up and down. She was wearing another suit and some black pumps. He'd hoped she would have changed so he could see more of her figure.

Sage noticed Ian staring and replied, "I hope what I'm wearing is sufficient? I didn't have time to change." She lied.

"You're fine." Ian patted her knee.

At the touch of his hand, Sage could swear an electric charge passed between them. As soon as she had what she needed, she intended to end the evening as quickly as possible.

The maître d' at Jean Georges on Central Park West seated them quickly. Clearly, he knew who Ian Lawrence was.

"Do you like?" Ian asked, once they were seated.

"It's lovely." The restaurant was bright from the large windows with glimpses of Central Park and done in a beige palette that was unobtrusive.

A bucket of champagne was sent over almost immediately as if there was some cue between Ian and the staff. The waiter poured each of them a glass. When he was finished, he handed Sage one. She didn't recall mentioning she was thirsty, but then again, this was probably how Ian lived, champagne and caviar every night. It was very far from Sage's humble beginnings although she had acquired a taste for the finer things in life over the years. She'd even made significant strides in paying off the huge student loan from law school hanging over her head; if she made partner soon, she would be able to pay it off in full.

To keep things professional, Sage pulled out her recorder. "Tell me about Lucas Johnson."

"You don't waste any time," Ian replied. She'd barely tasted her champagne and was all ready to jump in head-first into the deep end. "But I think the waiter needs our order first."

Sage glanced up and saw the waiter patiently standing by their table and turned off the recorder. After he'd taken the first and second course orders, Ian filled her in on Lucas.

"Lucas was always ambitious. He and I started out at Lawrence Enterprises at roughly the same time. My father was determined that I would learn the business from top to bottom, so he put me in a low-level position. I had to work my way up, the same as everyone else."

"And Lucas?"

"Was in the same position, our rise was almost tandem. If one of us got a promotion, the other was right around the corner."

"So it was a competition?"

He paused a moment. "You could say that."

Sage noticed how Ian chose his words carefully. "You didn't care for Lucas, did you?" she inquired.

"No, not at first," Ian responded. "I was bitterly upset that my father was treating me like the average employee after all he'd paid for my Harvard education. Plus my father lavished attention on Lucas, something he never gave me, so there was some resentment there. But Lucas was always a hard worker. I saw him in the trenches and we became friends. When my father passed away, I promoted Lucas to the executive level."

"What went wrong?" Sage inquired. "Do you have any idea where the racism that Lucas has mentioned came from?"

"I do. Bruce Hoffman, my bitter opponent on the L.E. board, is the culprit. He's a shareholder stationed in Los Angeles and despises me." Ian should have gotten rid of Bruce years ago, but he had too many friends on the board and Ian couldn't run the risk of alienating the board. Although Ian held a great deal of the stock, it wasn't majority interest. "Hoffman's hated me since the day I took over the company. Called me an upstart. Back to the case at hand—Lucas never reported the harassment, he let it escalate, but it doesn't matter. I will not let Lucas destroy my company."

"I see," Sage replied. The fact that Lucas never reported it was definitely in their favor. However, if there was harassment, Ian could still be liable.

The waiter returned and set her sea scallops with caramelized cauliflower and his sesame crab toast in front of them. "Please dig in." Ian nodded to the food.

Sage didn't care about the amuse bouche. She was dying to know what went wrong between these two respected colleagues, but she relented and took a forkful. "Go on."

Ian didn't respond because he noticed his deceased father's former girlfriend Gia Smith and another colleague walking toward their table. He hadn't seen Gia since she'd come onto him after the funeral and he'd thrown her out of his house and out of the company. He'd thought she was overseas. When had she returned?

Sage followed Ian's gaze and looked up at the beauty. Dressed in designer duds that must have cost a fortune, the woman carried herself with a regal air.

"Ian, what a surprise to see you," Gia spoke first.

"Gia." Ian rose and pushed back his chair. "What brings you back to Manhattan?" Truth be told, he was glad she'd been on the opposite side of the Atlantic in London. There had been less friction between him and Lucas without her presence.

"It's good to see you, too." Gia chuckled as she kissed both of his cheeks. "How are you, darling?"

Sage noted the familiarity with which Gia spoke to Ian. Clearly, they knew each other well.

"Well. And you? How long have you been back in town?" Ian asked again as he sat back down and perused her face. Time had been good to Gia; she looked as put together as the first time he and Lucas had seen her in the Lawrence Enterprises cafeteria all those years ago.

"I'm great. I've been back a few months. I'm working for Bob's firm." She motioned to her companion. "Bob McNamara, this is Ian Lawrence."

"We've met before," Bob responded and offered his hand. "Good to see you, Ian."

"You, too." Ian glanced in Sage's direction. "Gia Smith, Bob McNamara, this is my attorney, Sage Anderson."

"Your attorney?" Gia raised a brow. "Are you in some kind of trouble?"

Sage noticed that Ian didn't answer the charged question, so she extended her hand. "It's a pleasure to meet you."

"Likewise." Gia returned the handshake.

"Enjoy your dinner." Bob nodded at Ian and Sage before escorting Gia away.

"Who was that?" Sage asked even though she would

have preferred to ask if that was another one of his lady friends.

"Gia, Lucas and I go way back," Ian commented.

"Oh, really?" Sage asked. Now her curiosity was definitely piqued. "That's very intriguing, indeed. Maybe she can help your case."

"I highly doubt that," Ian returned. Although he knew they needed to discuss the case, it wasn't the reason he'd asked her to dinner. "You know the basics of the case, now I'd like some information. How long have you been at your firm?"

Sage wondered what about Gia had upset Ian so. She'd be sure to find out another time. "C'mon, like you don't already know," she said with a tease in her voice. She was sure Jeffrey had investigated her before Ian hired the firm.

Ian grinned. "Humor me. I would like to get to know the attorney who is representing me and whose shoulders millions of dollars are resting on."

"Okay," Sage conceded. "I've been at G.H.W.A. for nearly six years, I started clerking for the firm during the summer while I was at NYU and when I graduated, I was offered a position."

"So everything fell into place for you."

"Life hasn't always been roses for me," Sage replied. She reached for her champagne flute and sipped liberally. "Unlike you, Ian, I grew up with nothing."

"So you think I'm spoiled?" Ian asked. "Because of all this?" He waved his hand around.

Sage paused. "Spoiled has such a negative connotation. I would say you're—privileged."

"I would agree." Ian nodded. "But I have worked hard for the success I've achieved, as have you."

"True, but my success was a lot harder to come by,"

Sage argued. "Being one of the few African-Americans in law school and one of the few women at my law firm has forced me to work harder than the average male."

"I have a feeling that you thrive on it," Ian responded. Sage struck him as someone who wouldn't take no for an answer. When he'd finally read the dossier on her, it had detailed her successes in the courtroom. "I think we should toast to your success." He lifted his champagne flute.

"To success." Sage clicked her flute with his. "I suppose you have a point. When someone tells me I can't do something or a case is not winnable, I work extra hard to prove them wrong."

"Like when your boss thinks you can't secure a certain high-profile lawsuit?" he offered.

Sage couldn't resist smiling.

"Your moxie is what got your firm the case, but it's not why I chose you to head my team." Ian focused his intense gaze on Sage and she swallowed hard. Tension formed tight in her belly.

"You must know the reason I chose your firm was because of you, Sage." Ian looked her directly in the eye.

"Look, our food is here." Sage nodded to the waiter who was holding his grilled beef tenderloin in a horseradish puree with crunchy potatoes and her parmesan crusted chicken with artichokes, basil and lemon butter in his hands. "Hmm, doesn't it look delicious?"

As soon as he set it down, Sage avoided eye contact with Ian and went straight for her knife, but Ian reached across the table and put his hand over hers. "I find you extremely attractive, Sage, and I think we would be great together."

The touch of his hand on her sent a strong current coursing through Sage's body and she quickly moved her hand away. "Ian, don't." She glanced around to make sure no one had seen him.

"Why?" Ian's brow rose. "We're both consenting adults."

"Because you're my client and it would be completely unethical," Sage returned.

"I'm not the only one feeling the pull. A moment ago when I touched you, I felt a connection and I know you felt it, too."

Sage shook her head. Despite how she was feeling she had to draw a line in the sand. "I don't get involved with my clients," she said more firmly, more so to convince herself than him.

"Then I'm just going to have to convince you otherwise," Ian said, cutting into his beef tenderloin.

"You think you're going to change my mind?" Sage asked. "You're dead wrong. Once I make my mind up, that's it."

"Quite frankly, I don't think you'll be able to help yourself." Ian took a forkful of tenderloin into his mouth.

Sage's brow furrowed into a frown. "Are you always this arrogant?"

"I would say I'm confident."

"I'm sure a man like you is used to women more than willing to join you in bed, Ian, but I will not be one of them."

"Not yet," Ian said. "But you will be."

His comment lingered long after they'd finished dinner and dessert and moved on to safer subjects like politics, business and *Craze* magazine, Lawrence Enterprises' latest acquisition. Eventually, Sage glanced down at her watch. It was getting late and she needed to get away from Ian for her own peace of mind.

"Don't tell me you're ready to call it a night?"

"It seems we've discussed everything relevant to

your case. So I kindly ask that you take me home," Sage replied.

"Come." He rose from his chair and held out his hand.

"I won't take no for an answer." He grabbed Sage by the hand and led her to the door. The Bentley was outside waiting for them. When had he had the time to call? Sage wondered as she climbed inside the car.

A short while later, the driver stopped in front of the 60 Thompson Hotel in Soho. "You're taking me to a hotel?" Sage asked when Ian escorted her out of the Bentley. She couldn't believe his audacity or arrogance that she would sleep with him after one night in his company. She snatched her hand out of his and started for the car, but Ian stopped her.

"That's not why I brought you here." Ian reacted quickly and held a hand over the door. "Come with me."

Sage regarded him suspiciously.

"Cross my heart." Ian mimicked his words with his fingers.

Reluctantly Sage followed him and was surprised when the elevator took them up to the roof. The roof was completely empty save for a single couch and cocktail table while dozens of flowers and candles of all shapes and sizes adorned the ledges. A small stage had been set up in the middle of the roof and a band sat waiting.

The Manhattan skyline served as a beautiful backdrop on this mild spring evening. The sky was clear and Sage swore she could see a hundred stars. "Is this all for me?"

Ian nodded. "I reserved the entire roof. I didn't want any interruptions."

"And they just let you have it for the entire night?"

"For a price, plus I know the owner and he owes me," Ian returned. "But that's not all. Here's your real surprise." He motioned to the stage just as Robin Thicke appeared.

"Ohmigod!" Sage's hand flew to her mouth. *Ian had brought Robin Thicke to serenade her?* "I can't believe you did this."

Ian grinned broadly. "What's money if it can't buy you a few perks?"

"And you just happen to know Robin Thicke?"

"I know a lot of celebrities," Ian replied. "I am in media. Now are you going to stand there gawking or are you going to have a seat?"

As much as she wanted to say no, Sage wanted to hear the R&B crooner, so she allowed Ian to lead her to the plush patio couch with half a dozen pillows and a cocktail table with a bottle of champagne and two glasses.

Once he'd helped her onto the couch, Ian popped open the champagne bottle and poured Sage a generous glass. "To romance."

"Is that what you call this?" Sage raised a brow because no sooner than the first strain of the music started, Sage recognized the song Robin Thicke was about to sing, "Sex Therapy." "I would call it seduction, plain and simple."

Ian shrugged. "Call it what you will." He sipped on his champagne. "But I play to win."

"And that is all I am to you, Ian. A conquest. And once you've conquered me, you move on."

"I doubt I would move on so quickly." Ian's eyes roamed her face. "Why are you so busy trying to hold all that passion inside? I think you have a lot of pent-up frustration inside that you need to let loose."

As if on cue, Robin sang the lyrics "stressed out, uptight, overworked, wound up, unleash what you got, let's explore your naughty side…"

"You don't know the first thing about me, Ian," Sage replied, taking a sip from her glass. "I know how to let go."

"Good." He rose to his feet and grabbed her hand, forcing her to her feet. "Dance with me."

When Sage paused, Ian replied, "Are you game?"

Never one to walk away from a challenge, Sage didn't hesitate for a second to remove her suit jacket and lay it over a nearby chair. "Let's go." She sashayed toward the stage and stood with her arms crossed waiting for him.

"All right." Ian smiled and confidently walked toward her. Sage steeled herself for the effect of having Ian's hands on any part of her body. His large hand reached out and grasped hers while the other gently placed her left lightly on his shoulder before sliding around her waist to rest just above her spine. He was tender in the way he held her, but possessive all the same. He slid closer until their torsos touched. Sage willed her betraying heart to calm down; she didn't want Ian to know how deeply he was affecting her. Could he hear her frantic heartbeat?

It didn't help that the lyrics to Robin's song "Sex Therapy" were so seductive. "It's your body, you can yell if you want to. Loud if you want to, scream if you want to. Just let me love you, lie right there, girl, don't be scared of me. Give you sex therapy, give you sex therapy…"

Ian swayed his body to the music and Sage easily slid into a comfortable rhythm with him. As Robin's voice swelled, Ian tightened his hold as if she was his most prized possession. Sage glanced up to look at him and came into direct contact with Ian's appreciative male gaze. Her breath caught in her throat and she had to force air down her lungs as he kept his cobalt eyes fixed on hers throughout the dance. He continued to lead her across the floor and in one swift moment dipped her.

When Sage glanced up and saw the intense passion in Ian's eyes, she assumed he was about to kiss her—she would have bet money on it—but instead he lifted her back up. Ian and Sage were gazing into each other's eyes and they didn't realize the music had stopped until they heard the band clapping.

"Ian, the dance ended." His arms were still resting on the lower half of her back and he seemed reluctant to let her go.

"I know," he said smoothly, before finally releasing her. "Did you enjoy it?"

"Yes, I enjoy Robin's music," Sage replied, barely hazarding a glance his way as she walked back to the couch. She wanted off that bloody roof with all the candles and flowers and champagne. She needed some sense of normalcy, but instead she listened as Robin Thicke sang several more of her favorite songs, "Lost Without U," "The Sweetest Love" and "Magic."

Truth be told, the dance had awakened her. She'd felt sexy and womanly, but if the reason he'd brought her there was to loosen her up, his actions had had the opposite effect because she felt tenser than ever. "Are you ready to go now?" Sage reached for her jacket after the miniconcert was over. When she fumbled putting it on, Ian slid her arms easily inside.

"After you, my dear." Ian smiled as he followed her to the elevator.

Soon they were in the Bentley again, gliding through the streets of Manhattan after Ian gave the driver her address. Sage surmised his investigation must have covered every aspect of her life, including where she lived.

"So are you tired of fighting it, Sage?" Ian asked, shifting to face her until his knee was touching her thigh.

"Fight what?"

"Your attraction to me. The band saw it tonight. No, make that 'felt it.'"

Hell, Sage could feel it now, but she wasn't about to back down. "Ian, you and I can't have a relationship."

"Who said anything about a relationship?"

Sage scoffed. "Oh!" Why should she be surprised? He was Ian Lawrence after all.

"I want you and you want me. It's as simple as that."

"Sex is never that simple." Sage moved closer to the window. She knew from experience. Sex complicated things. She and James had been friends at NYU, but the night their friendship had become intimate, things between them had changed. Soon they were lovers as well as friends. Both ready to take on corporate America and get married. Who would have ever thought it would end so abruptly?

"No, but it can be extremely enjoyable." Ian scooted closer until he had Sage's back pinned up against the window.

Her eyes fluttered and Sage knew what was coming next, but she had no place to turn, no place to run. Ian was so close that her thighs were warm and her breasts began to ache with need.

His large palm curled around her neck and he drew her face to him. "You have a deliciously provocative mouth and one that I think can give me immense pleasure," Ian commented, seconds before his mouth covered hers.

His lips were pliant yet demanding as they moved over hers, persuading her to open up to him. She tried to resist, but she couldn't help responding by parting her lips. The invasion was swift as he tantalizingly stroked her tongue with his, possessing her mouth completely. Sage knew she should pull away and declare his kiss unwelcome, but she didn't. Her eyes drifted closed and she curved her arm around his neck, succumbing to the mastery of his kiss.

His tongue went deep into her mouth in one long thrust. Ian didn't just kiss her. He made love to her with his mouth.

There was no other way to describe the way his lips settled firmly over hers, while his tongue thoroughly penetrated her mouth, discovering and savoring her again and again while his hands took liberties with her body. He slid her suit jacket off her shoulders and boldly caressed her waist and hip. Then they moved upward to mold and massage her breasts through her dress. His thumb feathered over the hardened peaks of her nipples and Sage let out a satisfied sigh.

When the car came to a halt, Ian released her and finally lifted his lips and said, "I've wanted to do that since the moment we met."

Sage sat up straight and pushed him away. She was furious with herself for having served herself up on a silver platter. Her breasts were rising and falling in rapid sexual agitation. What had happened to all the platitudes she'd stated earlier in the evening that she didn't get involved with her clients?

Sage reached for her suit jacket that had been discarded in the moment of passion. "I have to go." She eased on her jacket, grabbed her briefcase and reached for the car door handle, but Ian stopped her.

"You and I sleeping together is inevitable, Sage," he replied. "You should accept it and stop running from it."

"I know you are used to getting what you want, Ian Lawrence." Sage turned around to face him. "But that is never going to happen." She rushed out of the Bentley before Ian could say another word.

Once she was safely inside her condominium, Sage sagged against the door. Ian had gotten to her. He was so handsome and so virile. How had she gotten herself into this predicament and how the hell was she going to get herself out of it?

Chapter 4

The following Monday, Sage received a package from Ian, or should she say Jeffrey. It was a file from L.E.'s former counsel on the lawsuit. After reviewing the particulars, Sage saw that they had completed their own preliminary investigation and found that Lucas was treated fairly when he was relocated, but there was evidence of harassment in the form of racial jokes or derogatory comments made by an upper-level staff and board member, namely Bruce Hoffman as Ian had suspected.

Sage contacted the firm's private investigator Patrick Kelly to run a complete background check on Lucas Johnson and Bruce Hoffman. "I need to know all there is to know about these two gentlemen," she said, zeroing in on her main targets. "Bruce Hoffman despised Ian. And I can tell you that Myles Lawrence encouraged a competition between Lucas and Ian. I believe Lucas harbored some resentment because of it, but why would both these men suddenly turn against each other and Ian?"

"I'll get right on it," Patrick replied.

She'd just hung up when Marissa poked her head into her office. "Interested in some lunch?"

Sage glanced up. "I'd love a break." She was tired of reading the Lawrence file. She pulled her purse from her drawer, swung it over her shoulder and rose from her chair. "Let's go."

They headed to an American-style restaurant a couple of blocks away from their building. Due to the late hour, they were seated within minutes.

The waiter handed them both menus and filled up their water glasses. "How did your dinner meeting go with Ian?" Marissa inquired after she'd given the waiter her order.

"It was informative," Sage replied, handing him the menu. "I'll have the tomato basil soup and turkey club."

Marissa searched Sage's face for the truth, but her brown eyes were clouded. "Okay, what gives?" It was unlike Sage not to expound on a case.

"What do you mean?" Sage reached for her water glass.

"You know what I mean," Marissa returned, eyeing her suspiciously. "You told me you were attracted to Ian and that he had invited you to dinner. And all you have to say is it was informative? C'mon, there has to be more to the story, Sage."

Sage shrugged. "It was a business dinner, nothing more."

"Where did he take you?" Marissa pressed.

Sage rolled her eyes. "Does it really matter?" When Marissa raised a brow, she responded. "All right." She sighed. "We went to Jean Georges."

Marissa shook her head. "Sage, you're on dangerous territory here. This is the biggest case of your career. You can't afford to get involved with your client. You have too much riding on this."

"Don't you think I know that?" Sage asked. She'd thought of nothing else for the remainder of the evening after Ian had dropped her off. But she also hadn't been able to get the memory of that kiss out of her system either. There was no doubt that Ian had rocked her to her core and she was still feeling the sensations of his soft lips brushing across hers.

"I'm beginning to wonder." Marissa noted the glazed expression on Sage's face. "Did something happen last night?"

"Other than dinner?" Sage asked. "Nothing happened." She lied. She couldn't share the kiss with Marissa, because if she did, that would mean she was giving it credence, which she wasn't. She just had to chalk it up to being in the moment. It had been a long dry spell since her last lover and Ian had filled a particular need. "We discussed Lucas Johnson."

"The man who is suing Lawrence Enterprises?"

"Yes, and his rise to power at L.E. It was very intriguing."

"Look who's coming," Marissa said, looking over Sage's shoulder at two men walking toward their table.

Sage turned around and saw the opposing attorney, Brock Campbell from Sullivan and Watkins, and a slick fellow wearing a designer suit.

"Well, well, well, look who we have here," Brock Campbell said.

"Brock." Sage nodded her head at her rival. She was not the least bit intimidated by Campbell; she'd just trounced him in court. If he wanted another beating, she was ready to supply it. "This is Marissa Rodriguez. Marissa practices family law at G.H.W.A."

"A pleasure," Brock replied, leaning forward and shaking Marissa's hand. "Sage, I don't believe you've met my client Lucas Johnson. He's recently returned to New York after he was exiled to Los Angeles by Lawrence Enterprises due to harassment."

Sage glanced up at Lucas. So this was the man who wanted to bring Ian Lawrence to his knees? He wasn't bad to look at. He was tall, clean-cut and extremely attractive. Once upon a time, she would have found a man like him appealing, but there was something shifty behind his eyes that Sage didn't quite care for.

"I'll be handling Lucas's lawsuit against Lawrence Enterprises." Brock brought him forward. "Lucas, this is Sage Anderson."

"Ian Lawrence's attorney," Sage added.

The smug smile on Brock's face quickly vanished as the thought of facing her again in court came back into play. "What?"

"You heard correct," Sage replied. "G.H.W.A. has been retained as Mr. Lawrence's counsel."

Lucas, on the other hand, didn't seem surprised at the news. Instead his brow widened and a smile spread across his face. "I can see why Ian hired you."

"He wants the best labor attorney out there," Sage returned. "Isn't that right, Brock?"

"Hmm, I don't believe that's why." Lucas smirked, eyeing her up and down. "Ian always did like beautiful things," Lucas continued. "But a word of warning—you might want to be careful because Ian takes what he can get and when he has no further use for you, he discards you." Lucas inclined his head to both women and sauntered away, leaving Brock to follow him.

Sage fumed in her seat. The nerve of the man! She wanted to toss the glass of ice water in his face. "That bastard!" she said when they were no longer within earshot.

"He does have a point." Marissa shrugged after the two gentlemen had gone. "Ian is interested in you."

"Ian may have hired me because of the way I look, but I'm a damn good attorney and I'll prove it. Lucas won't even see me coming."

"You seem very pleased with yourself this morning," Jeffrey commented to Ian as they sat eating breakfast on the hotel terrace. It was a beautiful morning with hardly a cloud in the sky, unseasonably warm for April in Manhattan.

Ian smiled broadly. "I am. Everything is going along smoothly." He cut into his Greek omelet and ate a generous helping.

"I take it you mean your seduction of Ms. Anderson?" Jeffrey asked, bringing his coffee cup to his lips. "I must tell you, Ian, I think it's a really bad idea to get involved with your lead counsel."

"I heard you the first time," Ian returned sternly, wiping his mouth with his napkin. "But the attraction is not one-sided as evidenced by Friday night."

"What happened?"

"Which part?"

"Just spit it out," Jeffrey said, biting his piece of whole-wheat toast.

"Oh, maybe you mean the part when Gia Smith walked into Jean Georges with Bob McNamara on her arm?"

"Gia is back in the States?" Jeffrey asked. Although he'd been working at another firm, he remembered the tension the woman had caused between Lucas and Ian all those years ago. She'd torn a rift between the two men that only time had healed, or so they'd thought. "Our last report on her about a year ago or so still had her stationed in London.

This would explain why Lucas is all fired up. Lucas was always trying to prove he was worthy of her. What better way than to beat you."

"Out of millions," Ian returned. "But I won't let that happen, especially not with Sage at my side."

"So she's succumbing to your charms."

"Oh, yes." Ian smiled. "We had a romantic dance on Friday and one thing led to another…" Ian let the words dangle in the air and reached for his orange juice.

"So you slept with her?"

Ian sighed. "No. But her kiss was explosive. It won't be long before Sage Anderson is in my bed."

Sage was researching case law later that morning when her direct line rang. "Sage Anderson," she said absently, picking up the receiver.

"Hard at work?" Ian asked from the other end. He was perusing several magazine figures when he'd thought of Sage and couldn't resist picking up the phone. He had to see her again.

"Who is this?" She knew who it was, but she wasn't about to let Ian know that she would recognize his voice anywhere. The smooth sexy timbre of his voice was impossible to forget.

Ian smiled on the other end of the phone. "It's Ian."

"Mr. Lawrence, what can I do for you?"

"Sage, don't you think after Friday night we're beyond salutations?"

She supposed he had a point, but she needed boundaries. "I met the plaintiff at lunch yesterday."

"You met Lucas?"

"Yes, he was with his attorney, Brock Campbell. Campbell is shrewd, but I'll make mincemeat of him."

"You sound awfully confident."

"I am. I just beat Brock on our last case."

"You certainly don't lack confidence." That was what Ian admired about her—her ability to go after what she wanted despite the odds. He'd seen it that first time they'd met when she'd sneaked into his suite.

"It's the reason you hired me, is it not?"

Ian paused on the other end. It was one of the reasons. "Of course."

Sage doubted it, but asked, "Was there a reason for your call?"

Ian smiled inwardly because Sage refused to give an inch; she had to call the shots. "Yes, there is. As I told you the other night, I'm relaunching *Craze,* the latest acquisition to the Lawrence Enterprises brand. *Craze* is a lifestyle magazine similar to *Essence*."

"And?"

"I'd like to invite you to the launch party on Saturday. I've chartered a private yacht for the evening and we'll cruise the Hudson River. There will be a dance floor, plus all the champagne and all the appetizers you can stand."

"I'll be busy working on your case."

"You can't work all the time and the party *is* on the weekend."

"I clock over seventy hours a week, Ian, which means I work weekends."

"Well, then look at this as an opportunity."

"An opportunity for what?"

"To gain insight into L.E. should I choose Greenberg, Hanson, Waggoner and Associates to take over as my corporate counsel once this case is resolved."

Sage wanted to scream. Of course, he'd dangle the bait of hiring her firm permanently to lure her into his web. She should resist, but the chance to get the firm's foot in the door was impossible to resist as he knew it would be. "All right," Sage conceded. "What time should I be there?"

"The cruise leaves at 6:00 p.m."

"Fine. Count me in," Sage said and hung up the phone. Now all she had to do was find a date. Unfortunately, her black book was pretty small these days. As she'd told Ian, she rarely had time for a social life, which meant she was going to need one of the men in her life to fill in and she knew exactly who to ask.

Shortly after 7:00 p.m., Sage strolled into the Henri Lawrence Gallery in Soho. Quentin's fiancée, Avery Roberts, was a buyer at the gallery and having an art showing that evening to introduce her latest protégé. Sage smiled as she watched Avery work the room in her usual poised fashion.

Avery was breathtakingly beautiful in every sense of the word. Tall, slender, with striking green eyes and wearing a high-waisted dress with a black upper bodice and plaid bottom, Avery was the epitome of class. Sage would never have thought Quentin would have gone for the ice princess, but he'd proven them wrong. When she, Malik and Dante had made a bet over a year ago that Quentin couldn't melt Avery's heart after crashing one of her showings, Sage was sure he'd lose. She'd been wrong. Quentin had not only melted her heart, but he'd also fallen in love and now they were to be married in three months. And along the way, they'd all discovered Avery to have a warm center underneath that cool exterior.

Sage nodded at Avery as she made her way to the bar where Quentin stood admiring his fiancée. "Q." Sage planted a kiss on his cheek.

"Sage, I'm surprised to see you here," Quentin said. "I thought the firm had you shackled to your desk."

"Ha-ha." Sage chuckled. "They do allow me to come out for bread and water."

"I'm glad you could make it. I'm sure Avery will appreciate your support." He glanced adoringly at his fiancée.

"What'll you have?" the bartender asked Sage.

"An appletini, please." She plopped her clutch on the bar.

"Put it on my tab," Quentin told the bartender.

"Sure thing."

Sage smiled. She could always count on Quentin to take care of her, which was why she'd come tonight. "I actually do have an ulterior motive for coming this evening."

"I'm shocked." Quentin touched his chest in mock pain. "You mean you didn't come out of the kindness of your own heart?"

Sage grinned. "I promise I'll purchase a piece if you'll agree to be my date for a work function I have on Saturday night." She accepted the martini glass from the bartender and sipped. She didn't expound that the work function was for Ian Lawrence. Quentin knew her too well. He'd already suspected that she might have more than a casual interest in the man and if she told him he was throwing the soiree, Quentin would surely give her grief.

"Sure," Quentin responded, tipping back his beer bottle and taking a swig. "Avery and I don't have any special plans, so it shouldn't be a problem."

Sage placed her glass down. "Thanks, Q." She gave him a quick hug. "You're a lifesaver. Be at my place by four on Saturday."

On Saturday afternoon, Sage stared at her sexy reflection in the mirror. The halter dress was perfect. The champagne color suited her complexion and the laser-cut tiers emphasized her shapely figure. The moment she'd seen it on the hanger at Bergdorf, she'd had to have it. It was a splurge at a whopping five hundred dollars. She'd told herself that she should wear something out of her closet and not dress up for the occasion, but the other side of her, the womanly side, wanted Ian to want her even though she knew a relationship with Ian was completely out of the question.

She'd gone to the beauty salon and her short hair was now a sexy mass of spikes. She finished the look with foundation, sparkly eye shadow and high-gloss lipstick.

"Wow" was all Quentin could utter when Sage opened the door.

"C'mon, it's not that unusual for me to dress up," Sage said when he walked into her apartment openmouthed.

"Yes, it is," Quentin replied, giving her the once-over. "Usually you're coming from work to Sunday dinner, so you're always in your work clothes."

Sage closed the door and thought about it for a moment. Quentin had a point. The last few times, she had come directly from the office.

"Well, you look fantastic." He kissed her cheek. "I'm sure several men will be lining up to get your number this evening."

There was only one man she was interested in impressing tonight, but Sage didn't say that. Instead, she eyed her friend up and down and replied, "You don't look too bad yourself."

Quentin was a handsome piece of sexy dark chocolate in a beige suit and crisp white shirt. Add the bald head with a diamond stud in one ear and the amazingly toned physique and Avery was one lucky woman.

"Thank you, thank you." He bowed. "Hopefully, I won't embarrass you too much tonight."

"You could never do that." Sage chuckled as they headed out the door. In fact, it was the opposite. She was hoping that having Quentin at her side would keep her from doing anything stupid that might jeopardize her career. The motto for the night was, Ian could look, but not touch.

The taxi dropped them off in front of the harbor and they followed the signs a short distance to a private yacht in the harbor. The party was already in full swing when they arrived. Sage could hear music bellowing from the upper decks as the crew helped them aboard.

"This should be fun," Quentin said, taking her hand. "Thanks for inviting me."

"You're welcome."

They climbed the stairs to the open-air deck where a large crowd had formed on the late sunny afternoon. Sage was glad she'd had the good sense to put on a little sunblock.

While Quentin went to procure them some champagne, Sage glanced at the view of the Manhattan skyline. She was so deep in thought that she didn't hear Ian approach until he was beside her.

Her obliviousness to his presence gave Ian several seconds to peruse her unaware and he liked everything he saw. The dress was sensational and finally gave him a chance to see her shapely figure. He wanted to run his hands from her curvy bottom up to her small but pert breasts that he'd love to latch on to.

Sage turned and her breath caught in her throat. Ian Lawrence was beside her and he was absolutely gorgeous. How was it that his peanut butter complexion looked even better in the elements? The linen blazer and trousers hugged his body in all the right places and tugged at her from deep inside.

"Sage." Ian smiled down at her.

"Hello," she managed to eke out.

"I'm glad you could make it."

Sage took a deep breath and found her voice. "Did I have much choice?"

Ian laughed and when he did, it was such a rich laugh that Sage felt it deep inside her womb. What was this man doing to her and why was he having this kind of effect on her? Where was Quentin when she needed him?

"Of course, you did," Ian replied. "And…" He moved so she could see her bosses, Mr. Greenberg, Mr. Hanson and Mr. Waggoner, standing several feet away. "As you can see, your presence is completely for your own benefit as I invited all of the senior partners."

"Thank you," Sage replied. "Associates rarely get the opportunity to schmooze with the senior partners."

"Then I did a good thing?" Ian raised a brow.

Sage smiled and, for the first time, she tried to relax. "Yes."

"Good, how about…" Ian was about to suggest they go someplace more private when a six-foot, bald gentleman walked toward them with two champagne flutes.

"Sage." Quentin handed her a flute and eyed Ian up and down. He was very protective of Sage and as he approached, he could tell the man's obvious interest in her, especially in the sexy dress she was wearing.

"Thank you." Sage accepted the flute. She smiled inwardly at the obvious jealousy spread across Ian's face. He in no way sought to hide his displeasure at the interruption. "Quentin, this is my client Ian Lawrence. Ian, this is Quentin Davis."

Quentin glanced at Sage questioningly several seconds before extending his hand. He'd been had. "It's a pleasure to meet you."

Reluctantly, Ian shook his hand. "You as well, though your name does sound familiar to me."

"Q's a renowned photographer." Sage squeezed Quentin's arm. "You've probably seen his photos in several magazines."

"Of course, Quentin Davis." Ian nodded in acknowledgment. "You do great work. You really have a way with the camera."

"Thank you." Quentin accepted the praise, but that still didn't mean he liked the guy. There was something authoritative about him that rubbed him the wrong way.

Sage was happy Quentin had come when he did, otherwise she'd be batting her eyelashes at Ian like some silly schoolgirl instead of behaving like a seasoned attorney. "Well, if you'll excuse us, I really should mingle with the partners." Sage grabbed Quentin's hand and led him away.

Ian was livid as he watched Sage walk away with another man. He'd wanted her all to himself tonight. This was definitely not how he envisioned the evening going. He would have to get rid of his competition and quick.

"What was that all about?" Quentin asked when he and Sage were no longer within earshot of Ian.

Sage played coy. "What do you mean?"

"Did you bring me here to make Ian Lawrence jealous?"

Sage's forehead wrinkled into a frown. "Of course not."

"That's not what it looks like to me. He wants you, Sage. And he was not pleased you brought me here tonight."

"I don't care what Ian wants." Sage turned to face the water just as the engines roared and the yacht pulled away from the dock. "He's my client, Q. You know it would be career suicide for me to get involved with him."

"That means absolutely nothing if you're as attracted to him as he is to you." Quentin grabbed Sage's arm and turned her around to face him so he could look her dead in the eye.

Sage lowered her head. She couldn't fool Quentin. "I can't act on those feelings. I brought you here tonight as backup so I wouldn't do anything stupid."

"And the dress?"

Sage colored.

"You're playing with fire," Quentin warned. "Even I know about Lawrence's reputation with women."

"I know, I know," Sage said. "I won't be foolish enough to put my heart out there for a playboy like Ian to stomp on. I remember all too well what happened with James."

"I could kill that bastard for hurting you." When Sage had told him James had cheated on her, Quentin wanted to beat him to a pulp.

"What's done is done. I will nip things in the bud with Ian before it gets started. I promise."

"I sure hope so, kid." Quentin pulled Sage toward him and embraced her.

Chapter 5

From across the deck, Ian fumed. He stormed across the floor to the bar and ordered a scotch on the rocks. As soon as the bartender slid him the glass, Ian downed the fiery liquid in one gulp.

"Is everything okay over here?" Jeffrey asked. He'd seen the dangerous look in Ian's eyes before and it wasn't a good sign.

"No." Ian turned back around so he could leer at the couple. "I want you to find out everything you can about Quentin Davis. He's over there manhandling Sage."

Jeffrey glanced at the couple. He didn't see any manhandling, but he wasn't going to correct Ian when the man was in a foul mood. "I think I still have the file on Sage in my briefcase. I believe the investigator mentioned him."

"Find it. I want to know all there is to know about my competition."

"Sure thing, boss." Jeffrey departed. He'd better get back quickly before Ian ripped the guy's head off.

When Jeffrey went to find his briefcase in one of the cabins downstairs, Ian turned back to the bartender for another drink and found Lisa standing next to him.

Her usual long weave was in a sleek, sophisticated updo and she was wearing a blue-and-yellow sequined strapless dress that with her long legs barely reached her knees. She looked ravishing. He could take Lisa downstairs right now and end the permanent hard-on Sage had given him since he'd met her. But as easy as that would be, he didn't want Lisa. He wanted Sage.

"Lisa, how the hell did you get on this yacht? You weren't invited."

"Ian, darling." Lisa leaned forward so that he could get a view of her cleavage. "You know I have my ways."

"I'll be sure to speak with the crew about that later."

"Now that I'm here, whatever are we going to do?" Lisa cooed. She remembered a time when Ian Lawrence couldn't get enough of her and a party such as this would send them both scurrying off to the nearest cabin and having sex like rabbits.

"*We* are not going to do anything." Ian searched the deck for a sign of Sage, but she had disappeared.

"Oh, c'mon, Ian, how long are you going to be angry with me?" She'd returned from Paris in hope that absence would have made his heart grow fonder. It hadn't. She'd been angry the other day when she'd walked out of his hotel room, but she'd had time to think and realized that she wanted Ian at all costs.

Ian turned to Lisa and found she was much closer than he'd like and rubbing her hand sensuously up and down his arm. He was about to dismiss her when Sage came back into his line of vision.

* * *

Sage shook her head in disgust. She knew she'd been right about Ian Lawrence. He was nothing but a scoundrel and a womanizer. No sooner than he'd left her side, Ian was talking to another woman, Lisa Randall, a supermodel to be exact. Sage guessed she shouldn't be surprised. Celebrities and models were Ian's M.O. Lucas had mentioned that Ian liked pretty things.

"Are you enjoying the party?" Sage asked Quentin, ignoring Ian. She'd had the opportunity to introduce him to her bosses and they'd all been impressed that Sage was friends with an artist of Quentin's stature.

"I am," Quentin said. The jazz band Ian had hired was wonderful. "But I doubt you are." He inclined his head toward Ian, who was whispering something into a leggy woman's ear.

"Who Ian Lawrence spends his time with is of no consequence to me."

"Sure, Sage." Quentin didn't buy for one minute that she wasn't the least bit bothered by Ian cavorting with another woman right in front of her.

When the band started playing the strains of Nat King Cole's "Unforgettable," Sage grabbed Quentin by the arm. "Let's dance." She couldn't stomach the way the woman was draped all over Ian.

Quentin obliged and they walked onto the dance floor that had begun filling with several other couples. They danced together as they'd done in their youth, when Quentin had taught her how to waltz for a school dance.

"Have I ever told you how much I appreciate you?" she asked, looking up at Quentin.

Quentin smiled. "Hmm, not recently, but feel free to sing my praises now."

"You're the best big brother a girl could ever have,"

Sage replied. "You've always been there to support me and I don't know if I thank you nearly enough. Without you and Malik and Dante, I would have never made it at the orphanage."

"You're welcome, kiddo." Quentin bent down and kissed her forehead.

Ian watched Sage look up adoringly at Quentin and it made him ill. He was unsuccessfully trying to ditch Lisa. Luckily, Jeffrey joined them.

"Lisa." He nodded at the model and gave Ian a questioning look. "I have that paperwork we discussed." He held up the file.

"Lisa, if you don't mind, Jeffrey and I have some business to discuss."

"Of course. I'll go grab a bite to eat." She smiled and headed for the buffet table. She was used to Ian dismissing her, yet she had a feeling it had more to do with the piece he couldn't keep his eyes off on the dance floor.

"So? What do you have?" Ian asked, turning to his friend.

"It's as I suspected."

"Well? Spit it out. Is Davis her lover?"

"Not from what that report says. Quentin Davis is engaged to Avery Roberts, an art buyer in Soho. He appears to be nothing more than a big brother to Sage, like the other two men she grew up with, Malik Williams and Dante Moore."

"So her carrying on with him right now—" he inclined his head to the dance floor "—is completely for my benefit?"

"I would say yes," Jeffrey replied. "And you bought it, hook, line and sinker."

"Not anymore." Ian stalked across the floor like a lion

ready to strike. Several guests tried to speak with him, but he had one purpose and one purpose only and that was to have Sage.

"May I cut in?" Ian asked. He didn't wait for a response and Quentin had to quickly step out of his way before he was knocked over.

Quentin was about to say something, but Sage shook her head, so he stepped aside.

Her almond-shaped eyes narrowed. "That wasn't very nice."

"He'll get it over it." Ian slid his hand in hers. "It's not like he's your man or anything. Isn't that right, Sage?" He pulled her firmly to him.

"Excuse me?"

"No excuses necessary." Ian's smoldering dark eyes were focused on hers, so much so that Sage had to look down. There was something dangerous and forbidden in them that Sage wasn't sure she liked.

"I should go." She tried to leave, but Ian kept his arms firmly around her waist so that there was no place she could move.

"Don't leave now," Ian replied. "Things are finally getting interesting." He spun Sage around and dipped her.

Sage swallowed hard. She felt the same tingling in her belly as she'd felt the first time they'd danced, except this time, it was much stronger. She needed to get away from Ian. When he brought her back into his embrace, Sage said again more firmly, "Let me go."

"Oh, you can go," Ian whispered in her ear, so that only she could hear him. "But you won't be alone." He bowed in front of the crowd and then lightly grasped her elbow and led her off the dance floor. Sage glanced around for Quentin to help, but couldn't find him in the crowd.

At the buffet table, Lisa slammed down her plate and

folded her arms across her chest. There was no mistaking
the look of hunger in Ian's eyes as he'd spun that wisp of
a woman on the dance floor. She knew the look because
she'd seen it in his eyes a hundred times before. It was clear
someone new had taken her place.

Sage had to nearly trot to keep up with Ian as he stormed
down the stairs; she was in three-inch sandals after all.
"Where are we going?"

He didn't answer. Instead, he led her down another flight
of stairs into what appeared to be his private quarters. He
opened the door, swung her inside and closed it behind
him.

Although the room was dimly lit, Sage could make out
Ian's looming presence and immediately stepped back.
"Why did you bring me here?"

"Isn't that obvious?" Ian asked, flicking on the switch
and flooding the room with light.

Sage glanced around and realized it was Ian's cabin.
There was a large queen-size bed in the middle of the
room.

"I don't know what you think is going to happen," Sage
said. "But I'm leaving." She started for the door, but Ian
blocked her path.

"Why leave?" He yanked off his linen jacket and
tossed it aside. "You have my attention now." His dark
eyes smoldered with fire.

"What do you mean?" Fear was knotting inside her at
the same time as the ferocity of passion. She focused her
attention elsewhere by looking at his broad shoulders and
massive chest.

He laughed as if sincerely amused by her confusion.
"The sexy dress—" he motioned to her halter dress "—and
Quentin."

"What about him?"

"Oh, c'mon, Sage," Ian returned, taking a seat on the bed. "It's just the two of us now. Just admit that you wore that dress and brought him here to make me jealous. And the display on the dance floor with you looking up adoringly at him was priceless."

"Quentin is my friend. No, make that a brother to me." Sage circled away from Ian until she was close to the exit.

"Right!" Ian stood up. "You wanted me to believe that you and he were more than friends. Well, you succeeded, my dear. I admit defeat." Sage had both angered and aroused him. She was unpredictable and different from all the other women he'd encountered. Most would be throwing themselves at him because of his wealth and social position, but Sage was doing her best to resist him and he had to admit it was one hell of a turn-on.

"Ian Lawrence admits defeat," Sage threw at him. "Why would you do a thing like that?"

"Because then I can admit how much I want you." Ian took a dangerous step toward her.

Sage retreated farther to get away from him until her back was against the cabin door. Her hand reached behind her for the handle, but Ian grabbed it seconds before he crushed her to him.

His mouth claimed hers, devouring its softness. Sage's calm was completely shattered at the hunger of his kiss and when he swept her weightless off her feet and onto the bed, Sage was lost.

His arms encircled her, just as his lips recaptured hers, but this time, they were more demanding than the last. Her lips seemed to part of their own volition and when they did, Ian's tongue dipped inside to explore the slick inner linings of her mouth. He continued his journey and dived deep into the hollows of her mouth. Sage moaned softly, lacing her hands around his neck and arching to meet him. He tasted so good and so uniquely Ian. Her mouth squeezed around his tongue and Ian groaned.

He felt exultant that Sage was reaching out for him. Whether she wanted to admit it, she wanted him, too. All her protests were pure stubbornness and he intended to have his way. The tips of his fingers caressed the satin softness of her neck, down and back up again. Then his hand crept lower and he softly stroked the side of her thigh.

"Ian." She whispered his name breathlessly and Ian took it as a sign of encouragement, especially when she pulled his shirt out his pants and slid her hand underneath it to caress his back.

With deft fingers, he quickly untied the knot at the nape of her neck and eased the dress down to her waist. She looked ravishing and utterly feminine lying there with her breasts rapidly rising and falling. Her breasts were perfect globes, high and round, but seeing was not enough. He wanted to taste them, to touch them and feel their texture beneath his fingertips.

His hand reached out to cup her breasts. He found them full and the nipple hard and it caused the bulge in his trousers to grow. Prying her hands from his chest, he slid them down to his torso to the fly of his pants and helped her unbutton the trousers so she could slide her hand inside.

"Please, Sage, touch me," he grated just as his mouth latched hold of one hardened peak and suckled. Sage nearly screamed when she felt Ian's mouth on her breasts. He was doing deliciously wicked things and she wanted to return the favor. Her palm enclosed around his shaft. He was hot, hard and thick. When she squeezed, he groaned out. "Yes, yes. Tighter, yes, that's it."

The incoherent chant went on until Ian had to have

another taste of her mouth and greedily ravished it. He was desperate with wanting.

Sage felt the same. Her breasts ached and the mound at the apex of her womanhood was throbbing with need. She didn't stop Ian when he lifted her dress, pushed her bikini panties aside and wove his fingers through the nest at her thighs. She was hot and slick and ready for him. Sage wanted Ian to possess her and he would have, if it hadn't been for the knock on the door.

"Ian, it's Jeffrey. It's time for the toast to officially launch *Craze*." *Knock. Knock.* "Ian, are you in there? Did you hear me?"

Ian paused from above Sage. Seconds before, Sage's eyes had glazed over with desire and she would have given in, but the knock on the door had killed the mood and he could see her mentally pulling away. "Yes, I heard you, Jeffrey. I'll be right up." Reluctantly, he rose from the bed and began zipping up his trousers.

Horrified by her wanton behavior, Sage sat up and pulled the halter over her heaving breasts. She tried to retie it, but her hands where shaking.

"Let me help you with that." Smiling, Ian came toward her as he pushed his shirt back down inside his pants.

"Keep away." Sage held up her hand. "I've got it." Somehow she retied the sash and quickly scooted off the bed. What had gotten into her just now? If Jeffrey hadn't knocked on that door, she would have had sex with Ian.

"Sage…"

Sage shook her head. "Don't say a word."

"We can't deny what almost happened just now."

"Oh, yes, we can," Sage said, adjusting her dress over her hips. "I, for one, am going to ensure this never happens again." Sage swung open the door and rushed out. When she returned to the deck, Sage searched the crowd for

Quentin. She found him by the bar having a beer. "I need to get off this bloody boat."

"We'll be back shortly." He inclined his head to the steadily approaching dock. "Did something happen?"

"Nothing I'd care to expound upon." Sage avoided Quentin's questioning eyes and stared at the water, which was much calmer than how she felt inside.

Ian returned to the deck shortly after Sage so as to not arouse suspicion and took center stage. He knew Jeffrey suspected something as he was waiting for him at the top of the stairs, but Ian was too much of a gentleman to mention that had he not interrupted them, they would have given in to the passion.

Sage watched Ian give his speech on his new magazine and what a great benefit it would be to the publishing community, but she heard none of it. Her emotions were a roller coaster. She'd just been saved from a very dangerous perch which she'd allowed herself to get on. As much as she denied it, she wanted Ian. And now that he knew she wanted him, he wouldn't give up his pursuit. The problem was, Ian Lawrence wasn't the commitment kind. If she allowed herself to give in to the all-consuming passion between them, how long before he tired of her? A night? A week? A month? Not to mention the potential ramifications if their affair was ever made public. She couldn't afford the risk. Somehow, she would have to find the strength to resist him.

Chapter 6

Ian was furious and threw the sales reports he'd been reading across the room just as Jeffrey walked into his office.

"Is everything okay?"

"No, everything is not okay."

Sage was avoiding him. She hadn't returned any of his phone calls in nearly two weeks. She'd even gone as far as to refuse the trinkets and flowers he'd sent to her office. She told the delivery boy to take the flowers to the hospital and donate them to the children's wing. Ian was not going to take this lying down. He was determined to have Sage and not even the woman herself was going to get in his way.

"Is there anything that I can do?" Jeffrey inquired even though he suspected Ian's foul mood had something to do with a certain five-foot lawyer.

"No." Ian rose from his chair. "I will handle this myself."

* * *

Sage was a realist. She had a battle ahead of her. Brock Campbell had a fire lit under him because she'd just beat him in court and didn't want another loss. She had to be prepared for war. She couldn't be bogged down with unnecessary emotions like getting involved with her client. She had to prove to the Lucas Johnsons and the Peter Waggoners of the world that she was not just a pretty face. Brains went with the body.

She threw herself into her work, reading case law and beginning the arduous task of interviewing some of L.E.'s New York staff. She needed to find out if there was any validity to Lucas Johnson's claim that he was passed over for a promotion and was relocated from L.E.'s corporate headquarters to a lesser office in Los Angeles where he encountered racism. Had Lucas, a senior-level executive, really been demoted with the relocation and his position given to a white colleague? Was that colleague paid more than him?

The HR department claimed the answer was no. Although Lucas had done a great job in the corporate office, relocating him was considered a promotion as that office needed a strong helm and Ian had felt Lucas was the right person for the job. His salary was commensurate with his title and Sage found nothing askew in what he was paid in comparison to his white counterparts. All of this was welcome news to her ears, but she still had the obstacle of Bruce Hoffman ahead of her. She needed to interview the accused and find out exactly what transpired between him and Lucas.

Focusing all of her energy on her case load had helped her wrangle herself free of a potential disaster with Ian. Avoidance was the name of the game. She'd ignored his phone calls and when she'd seen him once in the L.E.

hallway during her interviews, she'd ducked into the ladies' room before he saw her.

She was very pleased with herself and was smiling smugly when Ian burst through her office door one afternoon in the middle of May. "Ian!" Sage stood up. "What are you doing here? And don't you know how to knock?"

"You refused my flowers," Ian stated, shutting the door behind him. "And the necklace I sent." He'd been shocked when Tiffany had called to tell him that the Jean Schlumberger 18-karat platinum diamond bracelet he'd sent had been returned. He'd never had a woman turn down one of his gifts.

His tall, looming presence filled Sage's office and his intoxicating cologne wafted through the air, sending Sage's hormones into overdrive. She loved a man who smelled good.

"Yes, I returned them." Sage walked past Ian to her console and unscrewed a bottle of water. "They were completely inappropriate. I am not one of your little playthings, Ian."

"I never thought that you were," he replied. He'd enjoyed watching her curvy figure strut across the room. Although she tried to hide the luscious bottom he'd encountered on the yacht under a pencil skirt and matching jacket, Ian remembered. "I happen to enjoy giving gifts."

"Because it's just money, right?" Sage replied, spinning around. "You're used to throwing money around like it's water, Ian. I can't be bought with a shiny piece of jewelry."

Ian was stunned by Sage's reaction. "I'm sorry, I didn't mean to offend you." All of the women he'd encountered usually enjoyed the trinkets that showed his affection.

Obviously, Sage was different, which made Ian even more intrigued.

"You did." Sage folded her arms across her chest and walked back to the safety of her desk. He didn't see anything wrong because he was rich. Wealth was a lifestyle for him. It just went to show that they had fundamental differences and were worlds apart. "I hope you realize now that a personal relationship between us is completely out of the question."

"I refuse to accept that, Sage." Sure, they came from different backgrounds, but that didn't make them unsuitable. It just made Sage more of a challenge for him.

"You're going to have to because I've already compromised myself too much to begin with. Going forward, our relationship will be purely professional and if you can't accept that, then perhaps you should find yourself another attorney."

Ian leaned down with both his hands flanking Sage's desk and peered into her brown eyes. "Those are bold words for someone whose personal advancement hinges upon the success of this lawsuit."

"Which I will win," Sage fired back. "And I won't let anyone or anything jeopardize my standing with this firm. I've worked too hard to get where I am."

"All right." Ian retreated and stood up to his full six-foot-three height. Sage refused to give any inch, but he wasn't a man to walk away from a challenge. He would wear her down in time.

When Ian smiled at her, all of Sage's senses heightened and awareness of his arresting male presence flowed through her entire body. She did her best to act as if he had no effect on her. Her assistant saved the day by interrupting on the intercom to tell her that Dante was waiting to see her. Sage told her to send him right in.

Sage was relieved when Dante opened the door and her heightened color subsided because it marked the end of a highly charged conversation with Ian. "This is most certainly a surprise." Dante so rarely left his kitchen.

"If you're busy, I can wait," Dante replied, glancing at the other gentleman in the room. "I know I don't have an appointment."

"Like you would need one." Sage came forward and kissed his cheek and gave him a warm hug. Black slacks and a black polo shirt were his only attire, but Dante looked as handsome as ever. His hair was closely cut and his goatee and mustache were trim.

"Ahem," Ian coughed from behind her.

"Oh, I'm sorry," Sage replied and tugged Dante forward. "Dante, this is Ian Lawrence. Ian, this is Dante Moore."

"Nice to meet you." Sage noticed how Dante eyed Ian suspiciously.

"Likewise." Ian shook Dante's hand.

"Now if you'll excuse us, Ian."

Ian turned and glared at Sage. Was he being dismissed? After fully reading the dossier on Sage from cover to cover, he knew Dante, like Quentin, was not a threat.

"I'll leave for now," Ian said on his way out. "But we'll see each other again, real soon."

"So that's the infamous Ian Lawrence who has you all hemmed up," Dante commented.

"I am not hemmed up." Sage motioned for him to join her on the adjacent couch. "Sit."

"That's not what Quentin said after your cruise a couple weeks ago," Dante said, plopping down beside her.

Sage chuckled. "You guys are such gossips."

"Call it what you will," he replied. "But I know what I just walked in on and there was some serious sexual tension coming off the two of you."

"Okay, there is an attraction," she admitted reluctantly.

"Have you acted on it?"

"No!" Sage exclaimed but then backtracked. "Well… not entirely." The mind-shattering kiss in the car and the lusty session in his yacht cabin flashed in her mind.

"But you want to?"

"I don't." Sage shook her head.

Dante grinned. "Liar."

Sage's mouth broke into a smile. She hated that he knew her so well. "So what brings you here?" She changed the subject. "I can't recall the last time you visited me at the office."

Dante noted the switcheroo but answered anyway. "I'm interested in opening another restaurant."

"Oh, Dante, that's great!" Sage bounced up and down on the couch. "When? Where? What type of cuisine?"

"Slow down!" Dante held up his hands to fend off her questions. "There's a space in Harlem near Malik's community center that I love and…I was hoping you might help me negotiate the lease terms."

"Of course," Sage replied. "Like you have to ask? Whatever you need, I'm there."

"Good, I brought over the standard lease for you to review." He pulled out a large legal-size document.

Sage smiled. "I'll look it over and get back to you."

"Thanks, Sage." Dante rose and headed for the door but stopped when he reached the doorway. He paused for a moment.

"Was there something else?"

"If you want my opinion, you're entirely too cautious.

Perhaps you need to live a little and have a little fun. Maybe Ian Lawrence is exactly what you need. But whatever you do, don't fall in love with the bastard!"

After Dante had left, Sage thought about his parting comment. Was he right? It had been years since she was seriously involved with any man and she couldn't remember her last fling. After James, she'd shied away from romantic entanglements and focused on her career. Had it made her afraid of taking risks? And should she take one with Ian?

"How's your seduction of the lovely lawyer going?"

"Not too well. I need some time alone with Sage. Any suggestions?"

"Well—" Jeffrey rubbed his chin "—I would imagine she would need to interview some of the staff at Lawrence Enterprises in L.A. for the lawsuit, and while you're out there, you can look over that new acquisition."

"Hmm…" Ian thought about it for a moment. Jeffrey had a point. What better opportunity to seduce her than at his Malibu home? It was romantic and secluded. It would give him plenty of time to ravish her body and finally get the pint-size beauty out of his system.

He hadn't been able to get Sage out of his mind. The way she tasted, the way she smelled, the feel of her skin against his hands, the woman had completely encompassed his thoughts. Ian had never felt this way about a woman. He had never had a woman bewitch him like Sage Anderson had.

Women had always come easily for him. The problem was once he had his fill, he was done with them. But for the first time, he'd met his match. It made her irresistible.

"Sounds good. Arrange for us to stay in L.A. at the Four Seasons, then we'll head to Malibu," Ian replied and turned around. "Oh, and Jeffrey, make sure we have the penthouse suite."

"Consider it done."

"Good." Before long, Sage would be all his.

Chapter 7

"Ian Lawrence is looking into acquiring another holding for Lawrence Enterprises and he's asked one of our staff to accompany him to Los Angeles to consult," Elliott Greenberg said when he called Sage into his office for an informal meeting several days later. "And we'd like you to be that person, Sage."

"But why me? I'm already working on the lawsuit."

"Why not you?" Peter Waggoner peered at her long and hard, so much so that Sage gulped hard. *Did he suspect something?* "As lead counsel on the lawsuit, you're certainly more up to date on Lawrence Enterprises' business than any of us. Lawrence obviously isn't happy with his current firm and this just might be the opportunity we need to get our foot in the door. Plus, he requested you."

Ah, there's the rub, Sage thought. *He requested her.* This was all part of an elaborate plan on Ian's part to seduce her. He knew if he dangled his company's business in front of the senior partners, they would jump at the chance to become L.E.'s corporate counsel.

"You don't have a problem with that?" Peter asked because of Sage's less-than-enthusiastic response.

"Of course not," Sage replied. "I defer to the senior partners and will do my best to persuade Ian of the firm's capabilities."

"We have no doubt you will," Elliott replied. "While you're out there, you might as well get the discovery process rolling and interview L.E. employees about the lawsuit."

"I intend to do just that." Sage smiled on her way out of the door even though she was inwardly fuming. She wanted to rush over to the Four Seasons and call Ian Lawrence out on what a low-handed move he had just pulled. But of course that was what he would expect. Get her all hot and bothered in yet another argument and the next thing she knew, she'd be sprawled out on his bed and begging him to take her.

No, no, no. She had to think with her head and not her emotions. She had to think of Ian as one of her opponents in the courtroom and put the skills she'd learned to good use.

"I just heard from Peter Waggoner," Jeffrey told Ian later that morning. "Sage will be accompanying you to Los Angeles."

"You know I'll need you to stay behind here in New York and keep everything at *Craze* running smoothly."

"Of course," Jeffrey replied. Ian wanted the feisty attorney all to himself with no interruptions. Jeffrey just hoped this didn't blow up in his face. "The Four Seasons presidential suite is all set for your arrival."

Ian smiled. He'd stayed in the hotel several times and

knew the suite to have two bedrooms along with a fabulous view of L.A. and the mountains. "Well done."

Jeffrey shook his head. Ian may be pleased with himself, but Jeffrey felt as if he was playing with fire. But then again, that was Ian. He was ruthless and calculating when he wanted something. Jeffrey supposed that was what made him such a great businessman. Sage Anderson had no idea who she was dealing with.

Sage paced the floor of her two-bedroom Upper East Side condo as she waited for the town car Ian had hired to pick her up on Saturday. She'd spent the better part of last night packing her suitcase for the weeklong trip to Los Angeles, so why did she feel as if she was forgetting something?

She'd packed her files and reports on Ian's case in her briefcase, several suits for the day, a few casual outfits, a handful of evening dresses and two bathing suits. She was going to California after all. So why was she fretting so?

She told herself it was just anxiety over flying in a private jet, which Ian had insisted on. Sage would have much preferred a large commercial aircraft, but deep down Sage knew it wasn't fear of flying that had her wound up as tight as a grandfather clock. It was fear of a certain six-foot-three man with a killer physique, piercing dark eyes and the most sinful lips she'd ever encountered.

Sage touched her lips with her fingertips. Even though it had been a few weeks since the launch party, she still remembered the feel of his Ian's lips as they roamed over hers, remembered the pressure as he coerced them into parting, remembered the taste of him as his tongue merged with hers and it still intoxicated her. She had to snap out of it. In less than an hour, they would be sharing a cabin for an almost six-hour cross-country flight and she needed to get her libido in check. She was berating herself for allowing her emotions to run away with her again when her phone rang. It was the driver and he was downstairs.

The drive to the airstrip was fraught with anxiety for Sage as butterflies somersaulted in her stomach. They were worse than the first time she'd tried a case in court. *Get a grip,* she told herself. Maybe it was because she'd thought Ian would be in the car, and when he wasn't, she became even more anxious at the thought of seeing him again.

When the car finally came to a stop, Sage jumped out before the driver had a chance to come around. She was eager for some fresh air. She was sucking some much-needed air into her starved lungs and resting against the side of the car when a limousine pulled up alongside the car. Out popped Ian wearing jeans with a white pullover sweater and looking like the cherry on top of a sundae.

Oh, my, Sage thought, standing upright. "Ian." She inclined her head in acknowledgment.

"Sage." Ian smiled at her warmly and reminded her of the perfect set of pearly whites he had. "You're looking well," he added. His eyes roamed her casual attire of jeans, T-shirt and corduroy blazer.

"I didn't picture you as the jeans type," she replied.

"Then I would say you have a lot to learn about me," he said, motioning for her to precede him up the stairs.

The cabin was spacious with a long couch near one window and several large recliner seats on the opposite end. A minibar with water, soft drinks, sandwiches, fruits and snacks was already set up for their arrival.

"So this is how the rich and famous live," Sage said, buckling her seat belt in one of the recliner seats, while Ian made himself comfortable on the couch.

"One of the ways." Ian regarded her from the couch. He'd

noted that she'd picked the seat farthest away from him. But no matter, by the end of the trip he'd have her sitting in his lap. "Would you care for anything to drink?"

"Water would be great."

Ian rose and headed for the minibar. He cracked open a bottle of club soda for himself and handed her a bottle of Evian. When their fingertips touched, Sage felt a surge of electricity course through her. She was sure he felt it, too, because his eyes darkened. But instead of saying anything, Ian sat back down and made polite conversation.

"I'm hoping this trip will be productive." Ian leaned back and sipped on his drink. "I'm looking at acquiring an online magazine currently in the red and bringing it under the Lawrence Enterprises umbrella."

He wanted to make nice, did he? Well, two can play that game. "Greenberg, Hanson, Waggoner and Associates are eager to be of assistance," Sage returned. "And would be happy to guide you on this or any other transaction L.E. might have."

"I just bet."

"That is why you brought me here," Sage said, hazarding a glance in his direction. "For my professional expertise, is it not?"

"Why else?" Ian asked underneath hooded lashes. He wanted this woman bad. So much so that it was becoming increasingly difficult for him to sleep nights because of his recurrent unrelieved erection. He needed release and this week he would end his agony and sink deep into her wet heat.

Their conversation was polite for the first half of the flight but with an underlying tension in the air. During their lunch of cold cuts and pasta salad, they both finally relaxed and talked about music and movies. Sage even moved from her recliner and joined Ian on the couch.

They discovered that neither of them was much into chick flicks but shared a common love of drama and action. For music, their taste differed on rock but converged on rhythm and blues, jazz and country. Politics was where they went awry. The conversation became very heated when Sage realized Ian was a die-hard Republican, while she was a Democrat.

Sage sighed. Just when she was thinking they shared some commonalities, Ian went and blew it all to hell.

"Can we agree to disagree?"

"Fine." Sage returned to her recliner and folded her arms across her chest.

"Not fine." Ian couldn't resist temptation and rushed over. He swept Sage in his arms and kissed her.

"Ian, we can't." Sage tried to struggle, but her resolve faltered when Ian picked her up, guided her legs around his waist and fell back onto the couch. His hands roamed over her behind, pulling her firmly against his burgeoning groin, while his lips commanded hers and shot flames of desire through Sage.

She responded to his caress by grabbing both sides of his face and kissing him back. Ian eagerly parted his lips and Sage plunged inside, exploring the interior of his mouth with her hot, wet tongue. Ian moaned underneath her and Sage gyrated her hips against his bulging manhood and whimpered.

"Oh, yes." She whimpered as her center came against his groin.

Her little moans made Ian deepen the kiss. He wanted to have all of her right now. He flipped Sage on her back and was in the process of pulling off his shirt when the captain's voice came on the intercom.

"Please buckle your seat belts in preparation for landing."

Startled, Sage jumped up off the couch and returned to her seat, while Ian fixed his clothes.

"Sage…" Ian started to speak, but Sage lowered her head and refused to look at him. His face turned to stone and he faced the window. Ian shifted uncomfortably due to the hard-on that only Sage could vanquish. It infuriated him that she was denying the inevitable when he clearly could not.

Sage was thankful when the jet touched down and she was finally released from the small confines of the cabin.

A limousine was waiting for them when they disembarked and whisked them to the Four Seasons. Sage was quiet on the ride and thankfully Ian didn't press the issue. While he went to take care of the arrangements, Sage went to freshen up in the ladies' room.

When she returned, he headed toward the elevator. "Follow me."

Sage didn't like being beckoned but followed him inside nonetheless. She noticed that the penthouse button was lit up. "We're going to the penthouse?"

"Yes, do you have a problem with that?" Ian asked. "Or would you prefer to slum it in a standard room?"

There was no need for him to be rude and Sage was about to tell him so when the elevator came to a halt. She was overwhelmed when he opened the door at the opulence of the surroundings. It was very similar to New York and boasted a baby grand piano, fireplace, dining area and private balcony.

Ian surveyed the room, taking in the champagne and fresh flowers. Once again, Jeffrey had outdone himself.

"You arranged all of this, this entire trip—" Sage swept her arms around "—to seduce me." When he didn't answer she continued. "And I suppose there's only one bedroom?"

Ian rubbed his chin. "No, there are two, if you'd like to use one. But as you're already aware, I seek to rectify that, and after what happened on the flight, we won't need them both for long."

Furious, Sage swept past him to the adjacent bedroom and slammed the door shut. Sage glanced around and noted that the bedroom was decorated with more fresh flowers and chocolates on the bedside table. There was even a box of lingerie from what Sage guessed was some expensive boutique. The bastard had thought of every detail, Sage thought as she plopped down on the bed. *Was it inevitable that they would become lovers?*

"Are you going to stay in there all day?" Ian asked from the other side of the door, when after nearly an hour had passed and Sage hadn't left the confines of her bedroom. He'd already showered and changed and her suitcases were still outside the bedroom door.

"So what if I am?" Sage asked from behind the door. She had to look out for her own self-preservation and if hiding in the bedroom was the only way to avoid dealing with her attraction to her client then that was what she was going to do.

"You're just being stubborn," Ian replied. "Aren't you hungry? I know I am."

As if on cue, her stomach rumbled. She could use a bite to eat; the sandwich on the plane had done little to curb her appetite. She swung open the door. "Fine. We can do dinner, but that's it."

"All right," Ian replied, pushing past her to bring her suitcases into the bedroom. "Why don't you take a hot shower and I'll meet you in the living room. I have a few phones calls to make." He caressed her cheek on the way out.

Why did he have to do that? Sage thought as she stripped out of her clothes.

She emerged from her bedroom in less than half an hour wearing a simple one-shoulder black sheath. She didn't want to give Ian too much to look at. "I hope this will do," she said, spinning around.

"You'd look beautiful to me wearing nothing but a smile," Ian replied. He liked the way the dress molded to her hips, accentuating her curves.

Sage colored. Ian looked equally handsome and virile in his pressed trousers, shirt and sports jacket. It wasn't true what they said about clothes making the man. This man *made* the clothes.

"Let's go." He grabbed her hand. "I made reservations for us for at a great little Italian place."

Il Cielo was far from a little Italian place, Sage thought as she exited the limousine and took Ian's arm. From its sparkling lights that glimmered in the moonlight to the cozy lighting and ambience, it was a romantic spot for two lovers.

"This way, *signor,*" the host said.

They followed him to a secluded alcove for two. "Thank you," Sage said when he helped her into her seat and handed her a menu.

Ian ordered a bottle of wine before Sage could even offer an opinion. "How did you know I want wine?"

"I don't, but you'll love it. It's an excellent vintage," Ian responded.

Sage ordered the tomato basil soup and pollo ai funghi porcini, a chicken breast with mushroom sauce, and Ian ordered loup de mer alla griglia, Mediterranean sea bass with herbs.

The food and wine were wonderful, but Sage expected nothing less of Ian when he was trying to woo her. She, however, intended to stay strong in her resolve to resist his advances.

"When are we going to get down to business?" Sage asked when the antipasto platter arrived for them to share. "We did come to here to work and look at a new venture. Or was the acquisition simply a smoke screen to get me here?"

"Yes and no," Ian answered honestly. He had never hidden his interest in her and wasn't about to start. He filled her in on the details of the online magazine. The current owner wasn't interested in selling, but advertising dollars had dwindled and he was beginning to be desperate.

"He's trying some advertising sources that are currently advertising very heavily with L.E."

"And of course, they want L.E.'s business more than his?"

"Is there a touch of cynicism in your tone?" Ian asked. "This is business after all. Nothing personal."

"Is anything ever personal with you, Ian?"

"Why do I have a feeling we're not talking business anymore?"

When the waiter arrived with their food, it gave Sage a moment to pause before commenting. "We're not. You're known for loving 'em and leaving 'em. Why would I risk that?"

"Because the reward would be phenomenal," Ian responded, never taking his eyes off her. "And my reputation is completely overblown. I never lie to the women I'm with about my true intentions. Why do you care anyway? You don't strike me as the commitment type either. When was your last relationship?"

"Seven years ago," she admitted slowly.

"Why so long? Ian asked. "And what ended it?"

Sage paused before responding, cutting into her chicken instead and taking a generous bite. "My fiancé cheated on me because he said I wasn't at home. Now mind you, he was working just as hard as me. So he was not only a cheat, but also a liar."

"And after your fiancé?"

"My focus has been my career," Sage said. "I was starting out with G.H.W.A. and I had something to prove."

"So you've put your career over your personal life?" Ian reached for his wineglass and took a sip.

"You make that sound like a bad thing."

"It's not. You know where your priorities lie and you let nothing get in your way."

"It wasn't as simple as that," Sage replied. "James knew I wanted to be a lawyer when we met. *He* changed, not me. And now I'm exactly where I need to be to make partner." Sage sipped her wine. "And if I play my cards right, it's in my reach."

"I have no doubt you will. Would you like dessert and coffee?" Ian asked when the waiter came back to their table.

"No, thank you, I'm stuffed."

Once he settled the bill, the car took them back to their hotel. Sage was quiet on the ride up to the suite. She was sure Ian would like nothing better than to take their relationship to the next level, but Sage had no intention of doing so.

"Thank you for dinner. It was great," Sage said and quickly headed to her room to escape Ian's all-too-commanding presence.

Ian sighed. Sage could run for now but she couldn't hide.

Chapter 8

Sage kept Ian at a distance during the next few days that followed. She accompanied him as counsel when he met with the owner of the online magazine for dinner on Sunday, listened as he gave the man the alternatives if he didn't sell: go under or file bankruptcy. She dined with Ian and a fellow business associate when he needed a companion on Monday evening, but still she kept him at arm's length. The only fun she'd allowed herself was on Tuesday when she'd agreed to go out with Ian and see the sights of L.A.: Rodeo Drive, the Kodak Theatre, Grauman's Chinese Theatre, the Hollywood Walk of Fame and the big Hollywood sign in the hills.

During the day Sage had interviewed several of Lucas's colleagues in the conference room of the West Coast office of Lawrence Enterprises and for the most part, she'd found Ian's employees to be a good-natured, easygoing bunch. People who enjoyed what they did and loved the company they worked for. All of his employees had indicated Ian was fair almost to a fault and rewarded excellence. They would make great witnesses for the defense.

She discovered that Lucas Johnson had done a phenomenal job in the L.A. office even though he hated to be there. But she did find one potential bump in the round. Bruce Hoffman had had words with Lucas several times. Several witnesses attested that epithets and racial comments were used. What would have caused this sudden display of racism?

On Wednesday afternoon she set up a meeting with Bruce Hoffman. He turned out to be short, about five foot seven with a stock build and pasty white skin. He had silver hair and Sage imagined he was a sly silver fox with a Napoleon complex.

He thought the whole incident had been completely blown out of proportion. Sage had become perturbed when he'd indicated that he'd been in the business longer than she'd been alive. She'd slammed her notebook shut, stared him dead in the eye, leaned across the conference table and let Mr. Hoffman know in no uncertain terms that she would not take that behavior. Bruce must have got the message because he leaned back in the chair and cooperated.

Sage learned he'd been in the L.A. office for seven years since Ian stationed him there. He'd called Ian a pretty boy who'd sent him to Cali because he was a thorn in Ian's side. Bruce hadn't been happy when Ian sent Lucas Johnson, his whipping boy, to look over his shoulder. Bruce had been a part of L.E. since the early days with Myles, Ian's father, and felt *he* was viewed as the figurehead in L.A. by the movie studio honchos and didn't appreciate Lucas trying to take over.

Bruce admitted to Sage that he and Lucas had a heated exchange in which racial epithets may have been used.

Sage realized there was validity to Mr. Johnson's claim that Bruce created a hostile work environment.

"Lawrence needs to settle this with Johnson," Bruce had said on his way out. "If he gives him a few million, he'll go away like a good little boy."

Sage had stared back at Hoffman in disbelief. Here was a shareholder of the company advocating settling a lawsuit. Why was that? Sage couldn't put her finger on why Bruce had suddenly become prejudiced. It was almost as if he'd done it on purpose. Something seemed wrong and Sage intended to find out.

She was mulling over her next move when Ian stuck his head in. *Why did he have to look so darn handsome?* Sage rubbed her neck in frustration. He looked very powerful and commanding in his Italian suit which accentuated his yard-wide shoulders and broad chest. And the face, well, it was a face Sage couldn't forget—dark eyes that framed a handsome face, generous mouth and square jaw. She had to suck in a deep breath at the animal magnetism that emanated out of his every pore.

"I just met Bruce Hoffman."

"He's a real character, isn't he?"

"He's completely belligerent," Sage returned. The way he'd talked to her at the outset was deplorable. Sage could only imagine what he'd said to Lucas. "So what's on tap for tonight?"

Ian grinned. *So she expected to spend her evenings with him?* He was definitely getting to her. "I'm afraid an unexpected meeting has come up that I have to attend."

Sage tried to mask her disappointment. It was clear her presence wasn't required for this particular meeting. "That's fine." She turned and closed her briefcase. "I'll just head back to the hotel or maybe I'll go shopping."

"I can have my driver take you wherever you want to go."

"No, thank you." Sage grabbed her briefcase and headed toward the door.

"Sage?" She turned back around at the regret in Ian's voice. "I'm sorry about dinner."

"Don't be," she replied on her way out. "We are just attorney and client after all."

Ian was annoyed by Sage's comment. He was more than just her client and she damn well knew it. He didn't know how much longer he could go on pretending.

While Ian was off doing God knew what and with whom, Sage did a Julia Roberts and went on a shopping spree on Rodeo Drive. She returned to the hotel several hours later with a lighter wallet and several bags filled with a new outfit from Dolce & Gabbana, Jimmy Choo and Fendi shoes and a new Marc Jacobs purse.

Exhausted, Sage threw her bags down in the guest bedroom of the penthouse suite. It was well after nine and the suite was empty, which meant Ian was still out. It burned her to know that he could be with another woman after trying to get her into bed. She knew she didn't have any right to be jealous, but she was.

Kicking off her heels, Sage scooted to the top of the bed and ordered herself room service. In the midst of her shopping frenzy she'd forgotten to eat and now she was too tired to go back out. Before she knew it, her eyes drifted shut.

Ian sighed when he finally slid in the access card to the penthouse. He'd just shut the door, discarded his jacket and loosened his tie when he heard a knock at the door.

Who could it be at this hour? Ian was surprised to see

a hotel staff on the other side with a room service tray in his arms. "I didn't order anything."

The deliverer seemed confused and looked at his ticket. "A Sage Anderson ordered dinner."

"Of course." Ian motioned him in. *Sage hadn't eaten all this time? Had she waited for him?* His heart leaped in his chest.

While the deliverer set down the tray, Ian reached into his breast pocket for his wallet and procured several bills as a tip.

"Thank you, sir," the deliverer said on his way out.

Ian walked over to the guest room and knocked. He knocked several more times and when Sage didn't answer, he entered. He found her sound asleep in the clothes she'd had on earlier. Several shopping bags were strewn across the floor. Poor dear must have exhausted herself shopping. She looked so beautiful spread across the four-poster bed that Ian couldn't resist stroking her hair.

It had been a long time, if ever, since he'd ever felt such a pull, such a longing for one woman. The desire between the two of them had been building for weeks and he couldn't take it anymore.

Ian bent down on his knees until he was face-to-face with Sage. She was lying on her side and just within his reach. Her lips were full and inviting and he just had to have a taste. Leaning over, he softly brushed his lips across hers and when he did, her eyes sprang open. He did it again and when she didn't resist him, Ian kissed her again, but this time, he rose off the floor and joined her on the bed.

"Ian," she whispered through sleep-laden eyes, but he put his fingertips against her lips.

"Don't say no, Sage," he said huskily from above her as he stroked her hair. "I know you want me as much as I want you." And before Sage could utter another word, his lips swept over hers, passionately coaxing a response from her. He kissed her long and hard and deep.

Sage couldn't help moaning as the kiss electrified her, so much so that all thought of the risks to her and her career went out the window. Daringly, her hand laced around his neck and she kissed him back, pushing her tongue forward. Ian's lips parted and he slanted his mouth over hers possessively.

He encircled his arm around her waist and lifted her upright. In one fluid motion, Ian was ripping open her silk blouse to reveal her satin demi-cup bra. Ian quickly reached behind her to unlatch her bra and it fell away revealing the beautiful B-cup rounded mounds he'd once tasted.

Ian drew an unsteady breath. "You are so beautiful," he said before his mouth came down on them, hot and heavy. He took one nipple in between his lips and sucked it, causing Sage to throw her head back in abandon. Then he drew circles around the sensitive bud with his wet tongue. He loved each of her breasts, drawing them into his mouth again and again like a hungry baby, that Sage clasped his head to her breasts. *How could she have denied herself such heavenly torment?*

Her heart was beating so fast and furious that she didn't realize Ian was unfastening her skirt until he was laying her back on the bed. Sage raised her hips so that he could remove her skirt and satisfy the aching need in her loins. He paused when his groping hands came into contact with her thong. He pressed his hand over her mound and felt her pulse quicken underneath his touch.

"Please, Ian," she begged. She wanted him and could wait no longer.

He answered by swiftly sliding the thong down her shapely legs and sinking his finger inside her. He found her wet and warm.

"Ian," Sage moaned when he began rubbing his thumb back and forth across her womanhood.

Ian watched as Sage squirmed and her teeth caught her bottom lip. "Tell me you want this. That you want me."

Sage nodded. "I do, I do. I want you inside me."

Ian didn't need any further invitation; he replaced his fingertips with his mouth and tongued the petals of her femininity with greediness.

"God, you taste good." He gripped her waist tighter.

Sage gave herself over to the short teasing flicks of his tongue and arched off the bed, raking her nails across his back as tremor after tremor engulfed her.

Once the convulsions were over, Sage realized she was hungry for more, so hungry that she reached for his tie. Ian bent his head and she pulled it over his head and flung it across the room. Then she was on her knees, yanking open the buttons of his shirt. He eagerly tossed away the garment and unzipped his trousers. Quickly, he slid off the bed and stepped out of his pants and briefs before rejoining her on the bed.

The curved muscles of his chest pressed against the pillows of her breasts and caused everything soft in her to yearn for his hardness. Her hands skimmed the flat panel of his stomach, going farther until she found the swell of his erection. Sage's hand clasped around the bulging shaft and teasingly stroked it.

She was about to lower her head, when Ian said, "Later." He separated himself long enough to find the condom in his wallet and protected them both. Unable to wait another second, he situated himself firmly between her thighs and glided into her silken heat in one fluid thrust.

Sage instantly felt filled and fulfilled. How could she feel this way when Ian was offering her nothing more than casual sex? But she couldn't help it; she felt satisfied. And when Ian grasped her hands and intertwined their fingers together as he thrust in and out, Sage couldn't think about the pain and disaster this would potentially lead to. She just squeezed her eyes shut and focused on the grinding, rocking motion of their bodies unified as one until Ian said, "Look at me."

The raw need in his eyes swept Sage away. He'd drawn her in deep and fast and she felt utterly powerless. He withdrew until Sage could only feel the tip of him and then he glided in again and the friction was nearly unbearable. He was slow and easy one minute and then thrusting harder and faster the next. It was an exquisite agony that Sage didn't want to end.

"Ian!" she called out his name as her body quickly built toward completion. He answered her silent plea with one final thrust and she burst into a million tiny pieces.

"Yes." Ian gave a shout as he, too, fell over the edge and the aftershocks rippled through his system. His lips brushed over hers before he rolled over to his side and glanced down at Sage. Her breathing was as rapid and shallow as his.

"That was incredible," he whispered in her ear. The way she'd cried out his name had made him come within seconds.

"Yes, it was pretty mind-blowing," Sage concurred. She had never been made love to with such frenzy and passion. Her sexual encounters with James, although sweet, had been wanting. And the few men since him had left her feeling unsatisfied.

"You sound surprised," Ian replied, brushing back her damp hair with his fingertips.

"I've just never…" Sage's voice trailed off.

"Climaxed," Ian offered.

Sage nodded. "Yes, at least not during intercourse. I

always thought it was me…that something had to be wrong with me because I couldn't let go."

"Baby—" Ian gathered her in his arms "—there is absolutely nothing wrong with you. You are an incredibly passionate woman. The men you were with obviously weren't doing something right. They should have tried harder to please you."

Sage smiled. He knew exactly what to say to boost her ego. "Thank you for saying that."

"I mean it," Ian said and when she tried to move away, he stopped her. "Look at me." He hooked his finger under her chin and forced her to look at him. The passion in those depths was undeniable and it reminded him exactly why he had to have her. "I don't ever want you to fake an orgasm with me, Sage. If ever you're not satisfied, tell me and I will make sure you are."

"Okay."

"Promise me."

"I promise."

"Good." He kissed her lips. "Because I look forward to discovering your body again." He reached for her once more.

Chapter 9

Sage rolled over onto her stomach to avoid the sunlight that was streaming in from the window. She was stretching out her arms when she came in contact with a hard male body.

Distressed, Sage turned over and sat straight up as remembrance of the night before came roaring back: Ian stripping her of all her clothes, Ian making mad passionate love to her, Ian making her come. Sometime during the morning, he'd carried her to his king-size bed and taken her and she'd come all over again. The lower half of her body throbbed and could attest to what an incredible lover he was.

Her movements must have disturbed Ian because he opened his eyes and smiled up at her. "Good morning, beautiful."

"Morning." Sage pulled the sheet over her naked breasts.

"What are you doing that for?" Ian said, lowering the sheet. He reached out and playfully pinched one of her nipples. "I told you last night I wanted to discover your body."

"Stop that." Sage pushed his hand away and scooted to the far side of the bed.

"What's wrong?" Ian rubbed his eyes as he sat up. He didn't like the look of regret he saw in her eyes.

"Last night should never have happened. I've completely screwed up everything." Sage shook her head. *How could she have allowed this to happen?* She should have resisted the attraction, but, oh, how good it had felt to give in!

"I disagree. Last night was great," Ian returned, grabbing her arm until she faced him. "Better than great." They'd come together harmoniously like two halves of the same whole. "Why beat yourself up? It was something we *both* wanted. Something we both enjoyed." Ian tried to pull Sage back toward him, but she resisted. "Life is too short for regrets, Sage. Why can't you allow yourself to enjoy this?"

"Because you're my client, what we did is wrong."

"What's done is done and we can't go back," Ian replied matter-of-factly, not that he would if he could. He'd wanted Sage and now that he had her, he wanted her even more and there was no way he was going to let any amount of ethics get in the way of that.

"True, but I can change the future." Sage threw back the covers to flee, but Ian jumped up and blocked her from leaving. He looked so magnificent standing naked before her that despite her protests, desire coursed through her veins. The same as the first time she'd seen him in the penthouse.

"No way am I letting you run away from me." Ian held her by her forearms. He could see her inner struggle;

feel how skittish she was. She wanted to ignore what had transpired between them. "Look at me, Sage." He crooked his index finger under her chin and forced her to look up at him. "Can't we just enjoy each other for however long it lasts?"

"Until you're bored?"

Ian grinned. "I imagine it would take a very long time for me to become bored with you, Sage. Anyway, you didn't strike me as someone afraid of a challenge."

"I'm not afraid."

"Then stay with me," Ian replied. "And not just this morning, but for the rest of the trip and after *if you want*."

"If *I* want," Sage responded, stepping backward. "Ian, an affair between us is rife with conflict. You must realize that."

"What I realize—" Ian lifted Sage in his arms and carried her back to bed "—is that I'm tired of all these words. There's no other woman in the world I want right now but you." And when he lowered his head and kissed her, Sage believed him.

Hours later after his hands and lips had explored every inch of her, they'd sunk into a silky warm bubble bath in the large tub and then slept curled in each other's arms.

When Sage finally awoke, it was nearly noon and she jumped up. Ian was already dressed in khaki pants and a polo shirt and smiling down at her. How had he managed that? Hadn't she exhausted him enough? Apparently not, because the man had a voracious appetite.

"Hungry?"

Sage nodded.

"I took the liberty of ordering up some lunch." Ian inclined his head in the direction of a cart with several plates. "I thought we should eat before heading on the road."

"On the road?" Sage asked.

"Yes, we're going to my home in Malibu. My car will be dropped off any minute."

"I don't recall agreeing to go to your home."

"You didn't," Ian replied, walking over to the cart and throwing a couple of grapes into his mouth. "But you'll love the drive up the coast, with the wind blowing through your hair, and the view of the ocean is nothing short of spectacular."

"Ian…"

"I already know what you're going to say, Sage, and I don't want to hear the reasons why this won't work. We have another few days here in beautiful sunny California before returning to New York. And I for one would like to enjoy them without you fighting me every instant."

Sage sighed. She would love some downtime; she rarely had time off working sixty- to seventy-hour workweeks at the firm.

"Just say that you'll enjoy this time with me, no questions asked."

He was asking the impossible of Sage to forget how dangerous this was and enjoy the moment. *Could she?* She paused. "All right," she said finally. "I'll go with you."

"Go shower."

While Sage dressed, Ian contacted Jeffrey to make sure the house was in order.

"Everything is just as you requested," Jeffrey said from the other end of the line. "Housekeeping tidied up and restocked the fridge with everything you could possible need and probably a whole lot you don't."

"Great!"

"So I take everything went as you planned."

"Everything is fine," Ian returned. They were actually better than fine, but if he admitted that to Jeffrey, then he'd have to admit that he was developing feelings for Sage and he wasn't prepared to do that.

With his silence, Jeffrey surmised it had. "All right. Well, I guess I will expect you back at the beginning of the week?"

"You can. And, Jeffrey," Ian added before he hanging up, "I'm MIA for the rest of the week. Don't contact me unless it's an emergency."

"Yes, sir."

Ian smiled. He wanted Sage all to himself for the duration and he didn't want any interruptions. He'd waited long enough to have the temptress in his bed.

She emerged twenty minutes later in a floral summer dress and espadrilles. Her short hair had been sleeked back to the nape, while her face was natural with only shiny lip gloss as her makeup.

Ian felt his groin harden. "You look sexy." He bent down and swept his lips across hers. She tasted sweet, too, like peaches.

"Thank you. So do you."

A short while later they were driving up the coast to his Malibu home. "You're going to love my house," Ian said as he whipped his Aston Martin DB9 Volante up the Pacific Coastal Highway. "It's right on the beach and on a clear night, there's a sky full of stars."

"Sounds romantic." Sage smiled over at him. She hadn't taken Ian for the romantic type, but then again, it wouldn't be the first time she'd been wrong about him. She was right that he was a fanatic about cars. The DB9 was one hell of a sports car, but with an understated elegance rather than a Lamborghini or Porsche which she'd figured him for.

The walnut finish interior and smooth leather seats were all beautifully designed.

When they arrived, Ian pushed a button on his visor and the gates swung open to a modern one-story home. Ian grabbed their bags from the backseat and walked up the driveway. As Sage exited the vehicle, she realized she had never seen a place like this before except maybe in the movies. The home was surrounded by walls of glass. The inside was bright and airy with stark white walls. The gourmet kitchen was state-of-the-art with stainless-steel appliances and opened onto a dining area with a fireplace and sophisticated entertaining area complete with a Mediterranean-inspired sofa and colorful pillows.

Ian dropped their bags. "So what do you think?"

"Ian, this really is beautiful," Sage said, turning around to face him. She circled her arms about his waist. "Thank you for bringing me."

Ian had been waiting to see that smile all day. "You're welcome and I'm glad you like it. I probably don't come here nearly enough."

"You should. It's an oasis."

"Let me show you another oasis." Ian grabbed her hand and led her to the master suite. It was nicely decorated with a king-size bed, fireplace and sheer white curtains. But the centerpiece was the sunken spa tub in the corner with a view of the Pacific.

"Nice touch."

"I thought so." Ian grinned devilishly. He imagined they would make great use of it.

"So what are you in the mood for?"

"Do you really need to ask that?" Ian pulled her toward the bed until she fell on top of him. "Because if so, I must have been remiss in showing you just how much I want you." He scooted back until his head was on the pillows.

Sage raised her dress so she could straddle him. Ian's hand immediately went underneath and was shocked when he found she wasn't wearing any underwear.

"Sage, you bad, bad girl." Ian tore the trifle of a dress off her body as if it were nothing more than a nuisance. If he'd known she was naked underneath the dress, he'd have stopped on the highway and would have probably taken her right there along the side of the road, which was probably why she hadn't told him.

"I know what time it is." Sage lowered her head and her lips came down over his. She welcomed the firmness of his lips and when she felt the sweeping thrust of his tongue, she grabbed hold of it and sucked voraciously. While their mouths fused, she reached for the belt on his trousers and unbuckled it. Her fingertips brushed his hard shaft as she tugged the pants and his briefs down his legs.

"Mmm," Ian groaned, kicking off his pants. He not only wanted to taste her lips, but he also wanted to taste her sweet nectar.

Ian gripped her hips and then slid underneath her to give her the most intimate kiss of all. Ian spread her outer lips and found Sage hot and slick and ready for him. He blew on the sensitive nub before flicking his tongue across it, her body involuntary jerked forward. Sage had to clutch the headboard to keep from falling.

"Easy, love," he said, spreading her legs farther apart so he could have complete access to the task at hand. He slid two fingers inside her, moving them slowly in and out, then faster and harder until he felt pressure building inside her.

"Ian…don't stop." Sage writhed above him.

Even though his penis was hard as a rock, Ian grabbed her hips and tongued her even more, until Sage cried out. "Oh, God, Ian!"

Let it go, baby.

He didn't stop until she started to shudder uncontrollably. Flipping her over, he quickly reached for a condom in his nightstand drawer. He ripped open the wrapper and protected them before lying back on the bed.

Sage lowered herself onto his waiting erection. She was so hot and wet; her body easily took him deep inside her. Their lower bodies ground together in unison, slow and rhythmic, until Sage said, "Any slower and I'm going to die."

"But, oh, what a way to go." Ian chuckled, sliding his hands over her firm buttocks and increasing the pressure. His mouth then found its way to her breasts and his teeth tugged at her rigid nipples, causing Sage to thrash and moan above him. He slid one of his hands farther to tease that sensitive nub at her womanhood and Sage exploded.

"Ohmigod!" Sage cried out as an exquisite climax overtook her and she fell over his chest.

White-hot sensations eclipsed Ian as a feeling of euphoria intensified then burst around him. He held her close, their bodies still joined until the spasms subsided.

When he finally released her, Sage was overwhelmed by the intensity of their encounters. He knew exactly the right spot to hit to have her crying out in ecstasy. She didn't recognize the woman she was becoming. Sex with Ian was exciting, spontaneous and erotic. The fact that Ian could bring that kind of passion out in her scared Sage. If she let it, she could become addicted, which wasn't a good thing. She couldn't forget Ian Lawrence was an infamous playboy who bedded women as easily as he took over magazines and television stations.

"How about a dip in the ocean before dinner?" Ian asked.

"Sounds perfect."

The rest of their day was as splendid as the beginning. A swim in the Pacific followed by a succulent seafood dinner at a small café along the beach and then more passionate lovemaking with the doors wide-open, the cool breeze blowing and stars in the distance. Lying next to Ian, Sage worried about whether she'd made the right decision getting involved with him. She slid from underneath his arm and out of bed. She snatched her satin robe from a nearby chair and wrapped it around her naked body and tiptoed outside to the deck to look out at the dark ocean. She was deep in thought when she felt Ian's presence behind her.

His arms circled around her waist and he rested his chin on her shoulder. "Is everything okay?"

Sage glanced behind her and feigned a smile. "Everything is fine." Sage turned her back to him and faced the ocean again.

"You're worrying about what's ahead. Can't you just enjoy the present?"

"I can try," she said sincerely.

"Good. How about we go back to bed? It's late."

"Sounds good." Sage took his hand and walked back inside.

As she drifted off to sleep in the safety of Ian's arms, Sage would remember it as a perfect evening to savor after their affair was over. Ian had not only been a giving lover that night, but a kind friend. What she didn't see was Ian leaning over her and watching her as she slept.

Chapter 10

Sage was having a delectable dream. She and Ian were making love, swimming on the beach, cooking steaks and bathing together in a big sunken tub. When she finally opened her eyes and realized where she was, Sage realized it was no dream. She and Ian had spent three glorious days in heaven at his Malibu home. But he was nowhere in sight. "Ian?" she called out, but no one answered immediately.

"I'm right here." He crawled back onto the bed with two steaming mugs of coffee. He was bare-chested and wearing pajama bottoms.

Sage couldn't resist touching his chiseled chest and brushing her fingertips across his nipples. "Thank you." She accepted one of the proffered mugs and brought it to her lips.

"You do realize I have to get back to work?" It was hard to believe it was already Sunday. The days and nights had flown by.

"Who says?" Ian returned. "You're with me. Your boss won't care because he'll assume you're here trying to woo me for my business."

"Which I haven't been doing a great job of." Sage smiled. She'd been too caught up in the man himself to care about business, which was completely out of character. "So, if we're not going back to New York, what's on the agenda for today?" He had to have something up his sleeve. Ian didn't leave much up to chance.

"Well, I thought we could spend the day aboard my boat," Ian replied. He had a forty-two-foot yacht he rarely used, but today was the perfect occasion. "You'll love it. Sailing is one of my favorite leisure activities. And the boat, well, it's got everything we need, a full-size kitchen, shower and a *bed*." Ian winked.

"Sailing?" Sage feigned a smile. "I don't know anything about sailing. The best the orphanage had to offer in the way of entertainment was a television and a broken-down ping-pong table."

"Sage, I'm sorry." Ian folded her into his arms. Sometimes he forgot how different their upbringings truly were. "I didn't mean to be condescending. I realize we come from very different backgrounds."

"To say the least."

"Don't be like that," Ian replied.

"Like what?" Sage asked. "You have no idea what it was like growing up with a drug addict for a mother who couldn't keep food on the table. You have no idea what it's been like to grow up with nothing, Ian. Me, Q, Malik and Dante—we learned at an early age to fend for ourselves, for every dime that came our way. Even with a scholarship, I had to work two jobs in college to pay for my books and expenses. I had to learn to be self-sufficient." She and Malik had done everything they could to stay in school, while Quentin and Dante started out at the bottom of their respective fields until finally making their way to the top.

"I have some idea about growing up with no one," Ian replied.

"What do you mean?" Sage asked. His father had been alive when he grew up.

Ian turned his back. "There's a lot you don't know about me, Sage. We have a lot more in common than you might think."

"Why don't you fill me in on the missing pieces?" Sage scooted behind him and tried to hug him, but Ian shrugged.

"It is common knowledge that my father raised me in his footsteps," Ian said with his back to her. "But what many people don't know is how he came to be a single parent."

Sage paused. "Your mother was never mentioned in any of the articles I read."

"That's because my father, being the multimedia mogul that he was, completely obliterated her from the picture," Ian said, finally turning to face her.

"Why?" Sage's forehead creased in a frown.

"Because…my mother had the audacity to run off with another man, a man with whom she'd had a former relationship. It was rumored that he could have been my father, but a paternity test proved otherwise. Anyway, when my father discovered the affair was ongoing, he gave her a choice—a life with her lover or a life with her son and him. She chose her lover."

"That's horrible." It was hard to believe a mother would choose a man over her own child, but Sage wasn't a stranger to it. Malik's own mother had chosen her abusive ex-husband over Malik, leaving him to be raised at the orphanage.

"It killed my father. He was a proud man and was offering her wealth and fame, but she chose a poor man over him. So he forbade all contact between she and I and sent me off to a boarding school. I was the youngest student there, but he didn't care. He just wanted to be rid of any reminder of her."

"And your mother?"

"I never saw her again. She was killed in a car crash with her lover a year later." Ian could still see the look in his father's eyes when he'd told him that his mother was dead. He'd had no compassion; he'd just been cold and matter-of-fact. His father had told him that love made people blind, which was why he'd been blind to the fact that his wife had been cheating on him. "My father couldn't be bothered with me. He left me at boarding school and when breaks or vacations came, he was nowhere to be found. I had a revolving door of nannies to attend to my every need."

"I'm sorry, Ian." Sage touched his arm.

"So you see I know what it's like to grow up without parents, Sage. Although my father was alive, he may as well have been dead like my mother because he was no parent to me. I raised myself."

"I guess we have a lot more in common than I'd thought," Sage responded and hung her head low. She'd had no idea he'd had it so bad. Ian came off as arrogant at times, but he understood the pain of feeling alone in the world. A pain that, although she had Quentin, Dante and Malik, was still acute and resonated throughout her life.

"That's what makes us perfect for each other." Ian bent over and kissed her forehead. "Because we don't need anyone or anything. We can fend for ourselves."

Sage frowned. Ian's statement was exactly the opposite of how she felt. It was because she'd had to fend for herself that she wanted to have someone in her life. She just hadn't been willing to settle. "Is that what you really think?"

"Of course, why else would you focus your attention solely on your career to the exclusion of all else?" he asked. He knew Sage hadn't serious dated anyone since she'd broken up with her fiancé nearly seven years ago. "You're like me. When you need affection, it's just a phone call away."

Sage inwardly recoiled. She didn't know why she was surprised at Ian's view of relationships. Look at what he had as an example. Of course, she didn't have a good one either. Yet despite it all, Sage believed everyone needed someone. When she'd met James, she'd thought she had someone to share her life with, but it wasn't meant to be.

And now here she was in bed with a man who didn't believe he needed anyone or anything. Sure, he enjoyed her body and all it had to offer and for as long as he wanted it, but why couldn't he want more?

That was when it hit her. Despite her best efforts to the contrary, she'd fallen in love with Ian Lawrence. Somehow he'd found a tiny crack in her well-maintained armor and slipped inside her heart.

"You all right?" he asked when she remained silent.

"I'm fine." Sage jumped off the bed. She couldn't let him see her true feelings, which was that she was crazy about him. "I think I'm ready for that shower."

"Would you like some company?"

Sage kept her back to him for a moment and thought about it. Should she end things right now and avoid further heartbreak, or should she continue to enjoy the little time they had left together? She chose the latter. "Love some." Because any time with Ian was better than none at all.

* * *

The drive up the Pacific Coastal Highway to Marina del Rey where Ian's yacht was located was beautiful. The sky was blue and the sun was warm as it beat down on Sage's back. Fortunately for her, Ian had been kind enough to lather sunblock all over her so she wouldn't burn in her print halter top, skimpy white shorts and espadrilles.

Sage licked her lips when she glanced over at him as he drove. He looked particularly sexy and rugged in a T-shirt and shorts. The shorts showed off his powerful thighs and well-defined calves.

When they arrived, the marina was already bustling with activity. Ian parked the car at one of the several docks and went in search of the business office to take care of the arrangements, while Sage unpacked the trunk with her overnight bag and a picnic basket filled with meat, cheese, crackers, fruit and wine.

"You ready?" Ian asked when he returned with the keys. Thanks to Jeffrey, everything was in order. The boat had been fueled and stocked with refreshments along with lobster, steak and the like.

"Lead the way."

He took the basket out of her hand and led her up the gangplank. "This is it." He stopped when they arrived in front of a boat called *Elusive*. "What do you think?" He pulled a plank from the side and walked aboard before leaning over to help her on board.

The name suited the owner because that was exactly what Ian was. *Elusive*. "It's lovely," Sage said, walking across the deck and looking over the main channel.

"Let me show you the cabin below." Ian scooted down the ladder with ease and waited for her below. Sage had to pay careful attention so that she wouldn't fall. Once downstairs, she looked around while Ian put away their bags.

The entire galley was done in rich oak and had plenty of cabinet space. Sage was surprised to find a front- and top-loading freezer-refrigerator, microwave and propane stove and oven. There was even a small seating area and stateroom with a bed inside.

Sage was a little nervous being on a sailboat and hoped he wouldn't ask her to help navigate. She'd been on ferries and large yachts, but she was a city girl after all and was used to having her feet firmly on land.

While Sage put away the items from the picnic basket into the fridge, Ian navigated the boat away from the marina. When Sage came back on deck, she sat in a nearby seat and asked, "How did you get into sailing?"

"Well, when you're in boarding school, you pick up a lot of sports you wouldn't typically, like skiing, tennis, lacrosse, snowboarding and of course golf. Most of my schoolmates would take pity on me and take me on their family trips. Thus the sailing."

"I see."

"It's made me into the well-rounded man you see in front of you." Ian grinned.

They spent the rest of the afternoon lying in the sun and listening to music on Ian's portable iPod station and sipping on wine and eating fruit and cheese. Sage couldn't remember when she'd felt this relaxed and this content. She was always working and proving herself to the senior partners that they hadn't made a mistake when they'd hired her that she forgot to enjoy life. Sage resolved to make the most of her time with Ian no matter how short-lived.

Ian, on the other hand, couldn't focus on sailing because his eyes were fixed on Sage and the teeny-tiny bikini she was wearing. The bottom showed off her ample behind and, well, the top left very little to the imagination. Ian smiled at the memory of his mouth on the round globes and bringing her nipples to hardened peaks.

As if she knew he was watching, her gaze locked on his from across the boat. It was an intimate caress and left Ian wanting to carry her downstairs to the stateroom and ravish her. But they were nearing Catalina, so his lustful thoughts would have to wait until a more opportune time.

Catalina was even more spectacular than Malibu. In only a few hours, they'd moored at one of the many coves on the island and were now picnicking along the beach after a leisurely swim. Ian had changed into some swimming trunks, allowing Sage to revel in his well-defined chest and abs. They were eating the cold cuts and fruits that Sage had packed earlier.

"That was delicious." Ian licked his lips. "And now I'm hungry for something else." He reached across the blanket they'd spread out and pulled Sage to him. He lightly brushed his lips across hers and when her lips parted, his tongue darted inside for a taste. He couldn't seem to get enough of Sage. The more he tasted, the more he wanted. He caressed her bikini-clad bottom and she moaned.

"You are making me so hot for you," Ian groaned.

"Then I'd better cool you off." Sage rose, pulled Ian to his feet and ran toward the ocean.

She splashed him several times before dipping into the cool, refreshing crystal-blue water and swimming farther out. When she emerged, she yelled, "You coming?"

Ian still stood along the edge of the shore completely mesmerized. With her hair sleeked back and the water glistening on her brown skin and lush figure, Sage looked like some sea nymph that had just risen out of the water.

Sage covered her eyes with one hand and brushed back her wet hair with the other so that she could see him. "Ian, did you hear me? I asked if you were coming in."

"Oh, I'm coming," Ian shouted as he stepped into the water. He couldn't wait to come and *in more ways than one*. When he reached Sage, she jumped on him, straddling his waist, and they began kissing passionately.

He tasted salty and manly, all rolled into one. Sage couldn't remember ever wanting any man as much as she wanted Ian.

"Let's go back to the boat," she said huskily.

"I thought you wanted to play," Ian replied, caressing her bottom.

"Oh, I do." Sage winked.

They quickly swam to shore, gathered the blanket and picnic items and headed back to *Elusive*. They had barely got down the ladder to the cabin before they were stepping out of their wet swimwear. They rushed toward the stateroom and joined each other on the bed.

Although they were eager to be together, their union was far from hurried. Never taking their eyes off each other, they sat upright and took time leisurely savoring each other's salty bodies. Nibbling, kissing and touching the other. Ian knew she was ready when he played with her womanly petals and found her slick and wet. He enjoyed teasing her, bringing her to a ripe peak and hearing her cry out his name with longing. When he felt she was ready to explode, he slid a condom on his enlarged shaft. Then he scooted Sage on top of him, wrapped her legs about his waist and slid inside her wet heat. Sage cried out in ecstasy as Ian thrust deep inside her and they came together as one.

His movements were slow and controlled, but as the pressure and intensity of their lovemaking grew, so did his movements. Ian's thrusts became quick in steady succession until neither could take anymore and they clutched each other in unison as an earth-shattering climax overtook them.

The intensity of their lovemaking seemed stronger than ever, maybe because they were facing each other and watching the other person's reaction. Sage was overwhelmed and apparently so was Ian because his body continued to spasm long after they'd come.

"Are you okay?" Sage asked, holding both sides of Ian's face.

"I'm fine." Ian glanced at Sage, but when he did, he saw such caring and compassion in her eyes that he lowered his head. He was a far cry from fine, but he wasn't about to tell her that.

Sage kissed one of his cheeks. "I understand," she said, kissing his other cheek. "It was pretty incredible for me, too."

Ian didn't respond. Instead, he remained quiet. Had she said something wrong? She must have because he slowly released her and extricated himself from her embrace. He rose from the bed without looking at her and seconds later she heard the shower.

Sage's heart sank. Had she revealed too much? Had her face betrayed her and revealed her true feelings? She always had a poker face in the courtroom, but matters of the heart were another story entirely.

"How was the shower?" She tried to sound cheery when Ian returned with a towel wrapped around his midriff.

"Great," Ian replied. "I feel rejuvenated."

He'd had a few minutes to think in the shower and they were going to have a talk. Just now after they'd made love, he was sure he'd seen—dare he say—*love* in her eyes. Having never had it, he wasn't even sure he knew what it was, but if it wasn't love, she was definitely developing strong feelings for him and that he couldn't have.

He'd thought the rules of engagement had been clear. Enjoy the moment, no commitment. He wasn't capable of offering Sage anything more. He'd never been able to before in his previous relationship incarnations, although if anyone was capable of making him want to try, it was Sage. But it was best she didn't get any ideas in her head or be further invested on a scenario that wouldn't come true. He wasn't capable of love because as he'd told her before, he didn't need anyone.

"Why don't you shower yourself and get changed." He kissed her forehead. "And when you get out, we'll continue our adventure." He'd prearranged an overnight stay at one of the hotels on the island.

"All right." Sage scooted off the bed and hurried to the shower. Although small, it did the trick and washed the salty ocean water from her sensitized flesh. However, it couldn't erase the fact that something had definitely changed between them the moment he stepped out of the shower. Sage just didn't know how she was going to handle it.

When she exited, she found Ian had changed into linen trousers and a pullover shirt. He was also zipping up his carry-on bag.

Sage's heart was in her throat. "Did I miss something?" Or were they over just as suddenly as they'd begun?

"No, not at all. We'll be staying at one of the resorts. You didn't honestly expect us to sleep on this bed all night, did you?"

"Actually, yes." Sage had assumed they would be staying on board the sailboat. "But thank God I was wrong." She smiled. Ian was nothing if not unpredictable.

"I am not that much of a masochist." He grinned, flashing those pearly whites she'd come to love.

"Glad to hear it."

* * *

They took a taxi from the docks to the Catalina Canyon Resort and Spa. Ian had arranged for a king spa room complete with a private hot tub for them to play in.

"It's lovely," Sage said when they entered the room. She walked over to the balcony and looked out over the resort. He'd left nothing to chance.

"I thought we could have a nice dinner on the bay," Ian said. "There's nothing better than a view of the beautiful waters and cliffs."

"Sounds delightful."

They strolled hand-in-hand along the bay, browsing in several boutiques before settling on a seafood restaurant for dinner. Although the service was impeccable and the food delicious, Sage noticed that Ian was withdrawn. She knew he was used to changing sexual partners frequently, but had he tired of her already?

"Is everything okay?" Sage asked, on the ride back to the resort.

"Everything is fine." Ian kissed her forehead.

Later that night in bed, Ian was just as hungry for her as ever and they made love not once but twice. He was passionate, yet giving—wanting to make sure Sage was satisfied. It made Sage wonder if she'd imagined his aloofness earlier.

The next morning, however, Sage knew she was right because Ian was already dressed when she awoke. No lazy morning with the two of them cuddling and kissing in bed. "Good morning, sleepyhead." He tousled her hair.

"Good morning yourself," Sage replied, throwing back the covers. "I see you wasted no time getting dressed."

He looked as sexy as ever in a T-shirt and olive-colored knee-length shorts. "We have a long day ahead, cruising back to Marina del Rey. I thought I'd get a jump start," Ian explained.

"Did I do something wrong?" Sage asked. "Because ever since yesterday afternoon, you've been acting distant."

"Was I acting distant last night when I kissed you here?" He leaned down and kissed her neck. "Or here?" He kissed the valley between her breasts. "Or here?" His hands traveled lower down her abdomen, but Sage halted him with her hand.

Sex came easy for Ian, that much was obvious. But show genuine emotion and he was ready to run for the hills. "I suppose not." Sage threw back the covers and headed for the bathroom.

"Are you angry with me?"

Sage spun around. "Why would I be angry?"

Ian sighed. "Listen, Sage..." He paused as if mulling over his thoughts.

Oh, here it comes, she thought, *the ultimate kiss-off.* "Say what's on your mind, Ian, what's been on your mind since yesterday."

"All right." He sat down on the edge of the bed. "I enjoy your company and I love having you in my bed. I'm just not looking for anything serious. I just want to have fun."

Sage put her hands on her hip. "Did I ever say that I was looking for something serious?"

"Well, no, but..."

"There's no buts," Sage said. "You've made your feelings abundantly clear on the subject and I'm content with the status quo. Okay?"

"Are you sure about that?" Ian asked, looking up at her, because she'd said that just a little too hastily for his liking. "Because you're standing awfully far away." Sage looked as if she was ready to bolt any minute.

"I'm sure."

"Then come here." Ian opened his arms.

Sage walked into his embrace. "Why are you bringing this up now?"

"Because…I don't want to mislead you into believing that anything more can exist between us than what we have now."

Sage nodded. "I thank you for that, but I'm fine." She bent down and brushed her lips across his. "Really, I am."

As he hugged Sage close around her midsection, Ian wasn't so sure he believed her.

Jeffrey called Ian while Sage was in the shower. He updated Ian on several pressing items at Lawrence Enterprises before asking, "How's Catalina?"

"There has been an unexpected wrinkle."

"Oh, really? And what might that be?"

"I think Sage is developing feelings for me."

Jeffrey shook his head on the other end. "Ian, I warned you about getting involved with your attorney."

"She's assured me that I'm wrong. That she understands the score."

"Okay. Then maybe you're projecting your own emotions," Jeffrey offered. "You could be seeing those feelings in her because you're developing them." Jeffrey had never seen Ian behave this way around a woman. Maybe he was finally starting to allow himself to feel true emotions.

"What?" Ian laughed derisively.

"Laugh if you want, but you've never cared about the feelings of any of your other women. Maybe I was wrong. Perhaps you should explore your feelings for Sage. She could be exactly what you need to be able to let go of the past."

Ian thought about Jeffrey's statement. He was absolutely

right. He typically kept his feelings in check. Growing up under Myles Lawrence's thumb, he learned at an early stage to keep his feelings at the door, because they wouldn't be tolerated or welcomed. But Sage was different. She wasn't like the Lisas of the world, those whom he could impress with power and fame. She'd had a hard life and expected a heck of a lot more out of life, out of her man. Even if she cared, she'd walk away from him just as easily as she had her ex-fiancé. Ian didn't want to dwell on that thought. He wasn't prepared for Sage to leave him. He hadn't had his fill. "How's everything on the East Coast?" Ian changed the subject.

"Well…I was going to wait to tell you about this when you got back, but Lucas has already started slinging dirt. He did an interview with one of the morning news programs about the discrimination he endured at Lawrence Enterprises."

Ian instantly became agitated. "That son of a…"

"I know," Jeffrey interrupted him. "That's why you need to get Sage back as soon as possible to do damage control."

"Will do." Ian hung up the receiver. It was time for their holiday to come to an end.

"What's wrong?" Sage asked when she emerged from the shower with a towel wrapped around her bosom. Ian's face was clouded with rage.

"We need to get back to New York, pronto," Ian said. "Lucas Johnson has fired the first bullet and we need to retaliate."

Within an hour, they'd checked out of the hotel and were back on *Elusive*.

Ian was an excellent boatsman and easily guided them back into the ocean and back toward Marina del Rey. Sage lay out on deck and let the warm sun rays and ocean breeze glide over her. She'd loved the outing to Catalina and the one-on-one time she'd spent with Ian.

He'd been quiet ever since she'd returned from the shower. He said it had to do with the case and they would handle things once on land, but Sage felt it had more to do with her growing feelings for him. She'd tried her best to hide them, but she'd fallen in love with Ian and what was difficult was the fact that although he desired her, wanted her, the feelings weren't reciprocated. It was her fault. She'd known from the start that he wasn't interested in a long-term relationship. But that didn't make it any easier to swallow.

When they returned to Manhattan everything would be different. They would no longer be lovers but attorney and client. Sage wasn't sure quite how she was going to make the transition.

Once they arrived back at the beach house, they quickly packed and Ian filled her in on Lucas Johnson's shenanigans in their absence. Sage was going to have to get her head out of the clouds and back to business. Her instincts told her that there had to be more to this whole scenario than Ian was divulging. How could their once-respectful relationship turn so sour?

His private plane was waiting for them on the tarmac when they arrived at the airstrip. She was sure Jeffrey had a hand in this, but it still amazed Sage how Ian could snap his fingers and people jumped.

Aboard the plane, Ian immersed himself in a hushed phone call on the sofa, while Sage made herself comfortable in one of the recliners far away from Ian. Better she get used to the distance than have cold water splashed on her upon their return.

When his call ended, Ian closed his cell phone. "Why are you sitting all the way over there?"

"I was giving you space," Sage replied. It was more the other way around, but she wouldn't admit it.

"Sage," Ian began, "I don't want space."

Immediately Sage sensed his rueful tone and looked down. She didn't want to hear that their time together was over.

Ian rose and kneeled at her side. "I know I was kind of harsh earlier, but really nothing has to change."

"What do you mean?"

"Once we get back to Manhattan, this doesn't have to end."

"You would like us to continue seeing each other?" Her heart sprang with hope although she dared not show it. Sage kept her face emotionless as she'd done in court. "I thought you didn't do relationships?"

"I don't," Ian said, but he also didn't want to lose her either. In the short time they'd known each other, Ian had grown very fond of Sage and of course there was the connection in the bedroom, which was unlike anything he'd ever encountered. "We can continue to enjoy each other so long as we both want."

"I see." Sage sighed. So nothing had changed. He hadn't come to the realization that he wanted more; he just didn't want to lose her as a bedmate.

"What do you say?" Ian smiled up at her.

Sage wanted to shout "NO" and tell Ian that she wanted more than an occasional romp in the sack; she wanted a committed loving relationship that would lead to more, possibly even marriage. Sage didn't want to be alone. She wanted a husband and a family someday, something she'd never had growing up.

Yet she didn't want to lose him. She loved him. "All right."

Ian cupped his hands behind her neck and pulled her forward into a kiss. "Good." He rose to his feet and settled back onto the sofa and pulled a file from his briefcase.

Sage watched him. It was so easy for him to go back to business as usual, but just how long would she be able to continue to deny her true feelings when her heart was on the line?

Chapter 11

Getting back to work Tuesday was much harder than Sage imagined. Gone were the sunny carefree days in Malibu frolicking with Ian on the beach or sailing off to Catalina on a moment's notice. She was back to the rainy spring weather of Manhattan.

Despite the great risk to her career, she'd agreed to continue seeing Ian once they returned to Manhattan. She knew she was playing with fire, but Sage was unable to let go of the man she'd come to care for so deeply. She loved his smile, his walk, the way he talked, his zest for adventure. Who else could have convinced her to try sailing? And then of course, he was a giving, passionate lover. The best she'd ever had. He always made sure she was satisfied, no matter the time, place or position. She had come a long way from a woman who just tolerated sex to a woman who actually enjoyed it. Ian had released the sexual being from within her. She hadn't been able to resist him and she looked forward to resisting him even less tonight.

Fate, however, was not on her side. One of her other cases hit a snag and she'd had to cancel her date with Ian.

The next day, it was Ian's turn to cancel, but he didn't do it in person. Jeffrey, of all people, called to inform her that Ian would not be available. Sage was livid. Was Ian reverting to his old ways now that they were back in Manhattan?

She didn't have much time to mull it over. After she'd caught up on her other cases, she called Patrick, her private detective that she had retained for the Johnson case, to find out what Lucas had been up to while they were gone. He revealed that Lucas had frequently been meeting a woman in secret. Lucas was going out of his way not to be seen with her by meeting away from Manhattan and in the wee hours of the morning. What was he hiding?

"Do you know who she is?"

"I'm working on it," he answered.

"Stay on it," Sage replied. "Perhaps this woman is the missing piece of the puzzle."

It was hard for Sage to concentrate on work when her emotions were swirling like a tornado around her. A visit to her physician to find out the cause of her recent asthma attacks had found her in perfect health. In fact, he'd determined psychological stress was most likely the trigger. She was definitely stressed now. Outside of the odd phone call, Sage hadn't heard from Ian, the client she'd made love to endlessly in California and who'd now carelessly discarded her.

The only bright spot in her horizon was the fact that Quentin and Avery's wedding in late July at The Plaza was fast approaching. She didn't feel like celebrating when her own life was in shambles, but as a bridesmaid she felt obligated to attend the bridal shower at Avery's parents' home that weekend.

Avery arrived looking as gorgeous and classy as ever in a white sheath with pearls. Her mother, Veronica, was every bit the New York socialite in a Dior suit and hat. Sage put on a smile and oohed and ahhed at Avery's gifts. When the appetizers were served, Sage passed. She hadn't had an appetite in days; that was what love did to you. It made her sick. Lovesick.

When it came time for her gift, some crystal flutes, Avery sparkled. "Thank you so much, Sage." Avery rose to give her a peck on the cheek. "These are beautiful."

"You're welcome," Sage replied.

After all the gifts were opened, Sage excused herself and left the house for some much-needed fresh air. She was looking down the road when she felt someone's presence behind her.

"How are you doing?" Peyton rubbed Sage's back.

"Not good." Sage frowned. "It's hard to see Avery so happy and not want the same for myself."

"Is there anything I can do?" Sage had been a lifesaver when her relationship with Malik hit a rough patch. Heck, it was because of Sage's meddling that Peyton had broken through the wall around Malik's heart.

"No, I just have to bear it," Sage replied. "Stiff upper lip, you know. I did it when my engagement ended years ago. I focused on becoming a great labor attorney and defeating my opponents in court. Except this time, it feels much different."

"Because you think he's the one."

Sage didn't just think it, she knew it. Ian Lawrence was the man for her.

* * *

Ian sighed as he stared out over Central Park from his patio Monday evening. His penthouse renovation was finally complete and he'd left the Four Seasons. Because of Lisa, he'd remodeled his penthouse to be more contemporary. He hadn't minded the masculine brown and cherrywood tones, but Lisa had said it was too depressing and had refused to stay for any length of time. So he'd relented. Despite his wealth, he hadn't been able to control an unforeseen lumber shortage or a delay in the manufacturing of the Italian marble for his foyer. He'd been homeless for two months longer than he'd anticipated as the construction continued, but now that it was done, he was home sweet home.

Unfortunately, after his and Sage's return, a big wrinkle in the deal he'd been cultivating for months in Los Angeles had nearly fallen through as the owner rallied to save his company. He'd had to leave New York unexpectedly for nearly two weeks. He'd salvaged the deal and now had a new online magazine to add to L.E.'s portfolio. However, he was sure Sage was furious with him for being MIA so soon after their getaway, which would explain why she hadn't returned any of his calls.

Admittedly, he'd been busy in meetings, but when he'd had a moment he had finally called. She was just being stubborn—not that it should surprise him. From the moment he'd met Sage, she'd been a challenge; she wasn't a woman to wait for greener pastures. She was a go-getter. It was one of the many qualities he admired in her, among other things.

It still didn't mean he wasn't bothered by the fact that they hadn't shared a bed in weeks. His body ached with need. In his meetings his mind would wander to the sleek curves of her body, her silky skin or the little moans she made when she was on the verge of coming. Ian missed

Sage even though he would never admit that to Jeffrey. Jeffrey was already ragging on him and telling him he was in love. Him in love? No way!

He wasn't some lovesick puppy. It wasn't in his makeup. He was a virile man in his late thirties. He had an itch that only Sage could scratch, plain and simple. The more he thought about it, the more he decided that he would not let Sage run the show. She may have done that in her other relationship incarnations, but Ian was determined to be in charge, to be in control, which was why he was about to show up at her doorstep completely unannounced.

"I brought food and drink." Dante held up a tinfoil container and a bottle of white wine that paired well with the variety of tapas he'd prepared.

"Thank you, Dante," Sage said as he came inside her condo. "But you needn't have."

"It's no bother," he said as he headed toward her kitchen in the rear with Sage behind him. "When you missed Sunday dinner, I volunteered to come and check in on you." Dante glanced at the frumpy sweats Sage wore and her usually styled hair was now all over her head. "How've you been, kiddo?" he asked, unpacking the food.

"I'm fine," Sage replied. She avoided looking Dante in the eye by finding the wine cork and focusing on opening the bottle. He'd know she was lying.

"As you wish." When she finally turned to hand him a glass of wine, Dante stopped what he was doing and grabbed her by the shoulders. Sage tried to look down, but Dante wouldn't let her. "Look at me. This has to do with Lawrence, doesn't it?"

Sage couldn't hide it from him and nodded. She hadn't seen Ian in weeks. Sure, he'd finally called her himself a few days ago, but how was she supposed to feel? After a glorious week in Malibu, he'd abruptly left for two weeks, leaving Sage to question her decision to become intimate with him.

Dante shook his head. "I thought a little fun might be good for you because you hardly ever date, but obviously I should have never encouraged you. You're in love with the bastard."

Sage's eyes teared up. "For the first time in a long time I feel a connection with someone. I thought I'd never feel this way again after James. The only problem is, I'm in love with someone who can't love me back."

"I could kill that bastard—" Dante got up from his chair and paced the room "—for being so cavalier with your feelings."

Sage stood up and grabbed his arm. "It's my own fault for falling into his trap, Dante. I knew I was setting myself up for heartbreak, but who could resist the wining and dining, the private jet and the beachfront house in Malibu? Add all of that romance and Ian to the equation, who let's not forget is incredibly good-looking, and you've got one hard-to-resist man." She laughed tersely.

"Even though he hurt you, you're taking the blame?"

"He didn't do it on purpose. I knew the score, what he was capable of, but of course we always want what we can't have."

"That still doesn't mean I don't want to permanently rearrange his face."

Sage smiled now because that was a Quentin-like thing to say. She shouldn't be surprised that Dante was all fired up to protect her honor. With Quentin planning his wedding, they'd gotten close in recent months. Dante was a great sounding board.

"Let's just eat." Sage pulled Dante toward the table. "I know now that a leopard can't change his spots." Ian had tired of her as he had of all the women he'd dated. Sage would just have to accept that and move on. It hurt, but she didn't have much choice.

They were enjoying their meal and wine when her doorbell rang. "Who could that be?" She wasn't expecting anyone.

"Considering the hour—" Dante glanced at his watch and it was after nine "—perhaps I should get it." He rose from the table and walked to the door. Dante peeped through the hole and saw Ian. "May I help you?" he asked when he opened the door.

"Dante." Ian extended hand.

Instead of shaking it, Dante glared at him.

"Dante, who is it?" Sage asked, coming down the hallway. She was shocked to see Ian standing uncomfortably at the doorway and her hand immediately went to smooth down her hair. She looked atrocious in sweats. Why was Ian here anyway? He'd certainly taken his time coming back to New York and contacting her.

"I hope you don't mind my stopping over." Ian stepped past Dante into the hallway.

Sage busied herself in the mirror by licking down the sides of her hair with her thumb, while Ian walked inside and glanced around her condo. She watched him finger several photographs on her mantels and eye some artwork on her walls.

Reluctantly, Dante closed the door behind Ian. He didn't like for one minute that Lawrence was there staking his claim.

"Actually, I do mind. So what do you want, Ian?" Sage asked, following him into the living room.

"Well, I..." All of a sudden, Ian felt tongue-tied and that had never happened before. He was used to speaking in front of people, so why was it so hard to tell Sage that he'd missed her? Maybe it was because her friend was staring daggers at him? It was clear that Dante was not a fan of his.

"We were having dinner before you interrupted us," Sage continued. "So if this is not important, I would like to get back to my meal. Can we meet at the office?" Although she had missed him, she wasn't about to roll over and play nice either.

Ian stared back dumbfounded. Was she really ushering him out? "I just got back from L.A." He found his words. "I thought we could spend some time together." Wrapped up in each other's arms, he thought.

"I'm afraid that's not possible," Sage returned. Did he think she was supposed to fall all over him because he'd finally decided to make room for her in his busy life? Well, he had another thing coming. She might love him, but she still had her self-respect. "I have other plans for the evening." Sage walked over to Dante and linked her arm through his.

"I see," Ian replied. "Well, I wouldn't want to disturb *your plans.*" Furious with being dismissed, he stormed out of the living room. Seconds later, her front door slammed.

"My, my, my." Dante laughed. "That was some power play. I'm impressed. I'm glad to see the old Sage hasn't completely left us." He tickled her in the middle.

"No, I'm still here." Sage smiled. "And kicking." Ian Lawrence would think twice the next time he assumed she'd dropped everything for him.

Ian was livid when he jumped back into the Bentley. He couldn't believe Sage had asked *him* to leave instead of Dante.

"Drive," he barked at the chauffeur. Sage had made

it clear she did not want to see him this evening. And usually he was happy about having his freedom, a night to be carefree, so why did it feel as if he'd just been gut punched?

Chapter 12

"**Y**ou will not believe the dirt I have on Lucas Johnson," Patrick said on the other end of the line the following afternoon.

"What do you have?" Sage asked. Patrick's company had been tailing Lucas for weeks now and she hoped he had something good.

"The mystery woman is Gia Smith, some hot-shot executive."

Sage remembered her because they'd met the first night she'd gone out with Ian at Jean Georges.

"And we learned that Gia Smith was Myles Lawrence's lover."

"You're kidding."

"No, apparently they were lovers until his death."

"Wow!" Ian had never mentioned a word of this to her, but then again, he was very closemouthed when speaking of his father. It was funny that on one hand they could be so intimate with each other in bed, knowing the other person's likes and dislikes, but yet on the other, they still didn't know each other.

"We spied Gia Smith with Lucas Johnson on several occasions, and just this morning, she was seen leaving Johnson's place well after two. And I have the pictures to prove it."

"Well, this is very interesting news, indeed," Sage replied. Why would Lucas Johnson be cavorting with Ian's dead father's ex-lover? Obviously Lucas and Gia had something cooking in the oven. "This is good work, Patrick. Thank you. I'll take it from here."

Odds were the couple planned this thing from the start to get back at Ian. For what, she didn't know, but where did Bruce Hoffman and a racial discrimination lawsuit fit in the picture?

She was reviewing her notes when her assistant poked her head inside her office and informed her that Ian wanted to speak with her. Sage assumed it was over the phone, but then the door opened and Ian walked briskly inside and her heart started beating rapidly.

Last night had given her pause to consider her feelings for Ian; she was evaluating whether to continue seeing him. She'd needed time and distance to think with a clear head, but it was clear she wasn't going to get that.

"Mr. Lawrence, it's great to see you. Please have a seat." She motioned to the chair opposite her desk. "Thank you," she said to her assistant as she exited the room and closed the door behind her.

"I don't want to sit down," Ian replied, coming toward Sage. "I just want this." He pulled her out of her chair, drew her toward him and planted his lips firmly on hers in a demanding kiss that robbed Sage of all thought. Crushing her to him, he pressed his mouth to hers. When her lips parted to protest, his tongue darted inside her mouth and probed the recesses of her mouth. When he finally lifted his head, she was speechless. "That's what I would have done last night but wasn't given the opportunity to since you had company."

"So what, you came here to take it?" she asked, pushing him and stepping away to fix her suit even though blood was pounding in her brain and her heart was racing a mile a minute from his masterful kiss. "I don't like being manhandled."

"Where is all this hostility coming from?" Ian asked. This was not the response he'd expected. "If this is about my not being available for a couple weeks, it was out of my hands."

"I am not that needy," Sage responded tartly. "You, on the other hand, are spoiled, Ian. You get what you want, when you want it. The world does not revolve around you. I have other interests and people who happen to mean a lot to me. I won't drop them just because you've decided you finally have time for me. And in case you've forgotten, this is a place of business. Anyone could have walked in on us just now."

Ian wasn't used to people giving it back to him. Jeffrey, maybe, but certainly not his woman; he respected Sage for voicing her opinion. "I'm sorry," he apologized. "I didn't think that you might have company last night. All I knew was that I missed you and I wanted you in my bed. Guess that was pretty selfish."

Sage smiled. Ian admitted he was wrong? That he'd missed her? He'd made some progress in getting in touch with his feelings. "I accept your apology. And actually, I'm glad you stopped by because we really need to discuss your case."

"What about it?"

"Who is Gia Smith to you, Ian? And what does she know about you and Lucas?" When Ian turned away and faced the window, Sage began to worry. "What happened between you two, Ian?"

"Nothing of any importance."

"Like hell." Sage grabbed his arm and forced him to look at her. "Why don't you tell me the real reason Lucas has a beef with you and how Gia Smith plays a part in all this?"

Resigned, Ian walked to the sofa and sat down. He'd hoped not to have to dredge up the past. A past that reminded him of his father, an unforgiving, cold man, who he constantly tried to impress to no avail, but apparently some things wouldn't stay buried.

"Gia used to date my father." When Sage didn't seem surprised, he asked, "You know about that?"

"Yes, I had her investigated. Go on." She didn't want him to get off track.

"My father liked beautiful things, as do I." He winked at her, but Sage didn't react. "And Gia was as young and beautiful as she was smart and ambitious. She didn't care that my father was twice her age. Gia saw dollar signs. My father was always a means to an end for her."

"So you tolerated her?"

"I did, but when he passed away, she seemed truly distraught, so I tried to be her friend. We became close."

"Lovers?" Sage held her breath. As his lawyer, she needed to know the answer, but as the woman he was sleeping with, she'd prefer ignorance. It wasn't as if she didn't know Ian to be a ladies' man, hadn't seen the pictures and articles in the paper, but it was another matter altogether hearing it firsthand.

"No!" Ian was surprised Sage would even think it. "I

would never sleep with a woman who'd been intimate with my father, but it wasn't for her lack of trying."

"So Gia is a woman scorned?"

"Oh, hell yes!" Ian answered vehemently. He'd seen right through Gia the moment he'd met her. She was an opportunist and when his father had passed away, he'd been the next best thing. "After her attempted seduction, I gave her a generous sum to disappear. And thank God I did, because at the time I didn't need that kind of headache. I was fighting with the members of the board and needed all my wits about me. From what I've heard, she's done well for herself in London, as I'm sure your report shows."

Sage jotted down notes on her legal pad. "And Lucas, what is his role in this scenario?"

"Lucas was in love with Gia."

"Really?"

"Yes." Ian nodded. "He wanted to marry her and thought after my father died, he'd finally have a chance."

"But Gia only had eyes for you?"

Ian nodded. "Yes. One night Gia, Lucas and I drank too much and eventually we retired to bed. I came down to the study because I couldn't sleep and Gia came down in a nightie and threw herself at me. Lucas must have seen her leaving my study and assumed we'd been intimate. He and I had a huge blowout afterward."

"But you didn't sleep with Gia?" Sage pressed.

"No," Ian stated emphatically. "I know everyone thinks I'm a playboy and some of the gossip may be true, but I never looked at Gia as anything more than a friend. But Lucas didn't believe that and after she left, he never trusted me quite the same. He assumed that I had tried to take the one thing from him that he loved most in the world."

"Why didn't you tell me all of this before?"

"Because it had nothing to do with the case." He'd dashed

Gia's hopes of becoming lady of the manor and despite the competition his father had stoked between him and Lucas, Ian had done right by Lucas or so he'd thought.

"It gives Lucas motive for fabricating these lies against you," Sage responded. "And if you must know, he's been secretly seeing Gia for some time now."

"You're kidding!"

Sage shook her head. "No. I think they've cooked up this elaborate scheme to get back at you."

"I just can't believe that it has come to this." Ian was furious as he stood up and paced her office. "For years Lucas acted as though it was water under the bridge, that he'd gotten over what happened in the past. Sure, we've not been buddy-buddy since Gia left, but I never suspected that he would be planning revenge against me and that Gia would be his accomplice."

"It happens." Sage shrugged.

"I'm going to take care of this," Ian replied and stormed toward the door. "There's no way I'm going to let the two of them get the better of me."

"Absolutely not!" Sage rushed toward him. She didn't like the fiery look in his eyes. She grabbed his chin with one hand. "Listen to me, Ian. You're going to let *me* handle this. I'm your attorney. I will get to the bottom of this whole fabricated story."

Ian smiled and drew her to his arms. "I like it when you get all bossy on me."

"Good, because I don't need you going off half-cocked and making this case any worse."

"And if I agree to that—" he lowered his head until he was inches away from her face "—can we get back to the way things were before we came back to New York?"

Sage lowered her head and laid it against his chest. She wasn't sure that was a wise idea. Ian would be under even more scrutiny now that Lucas had thrown the first punch. But Ian wasn't thinking about that; he was nibbling at the sensitive spot on her nape, sending shivers running right through her. "Ian, now is not the right time." She backed away.

"You're right." Ian straightened. "We'll finish this later. Can you meet me at my penthouse? The renovation is complete."

Sage closed her eyes. It was no use denying that she wanted to be in his arms, so she conceded. "All right."

"Excellent, I'll see you tonight."

After Ian left, Sage contacted Patrick. "Continue to tail both Gia Smith and Lucas Johnson and let me know what you find out."

Sage rubbed her hands together in eager anticipation of the battle ahead. There would be no holds barred on Lucas now that she was working with a full deck of cards. She would attack him with the same gusto she'd used on her opponents in the courtroom.

The fight was on.

"Sage wasn't too happy with me for being gone so long, but I intend to rectify that this evening," Ian told Jeffrey early that evening at the corporate office of Lawrence Enterprises as they prepared to go home.

"You know, I'm going to reiterate now that you're back in New York that I think this is a bad idea. What if someone sees you two? This can have a negative impact on her career."

"Duly noted," Ian returned. "Now can you set up to have dinner delivered to my penthouse at seven?"

"Very well," Jeffrey said and left the room.

Ian was reviewing the latest circulation figures on *Craze*

and his other magazines when his executive assistant buzzed him on the intercom. "Ian, you have a visitor."

"Who is it?" Ian didn't like to be interrupted when he was working.

"Dante Moore."

Ian turned away from his laptop and spoke into the intercom. "Send him in." What was Sage's friend doing at his office?

Dante walked in and, from the expression on his face, Ian could see it wasn't a social visit. "What brings you here, Dante?"

"I'm here to tell you to back off, Lawrence. Leave Sage alone."

Ian was taken aback. He'd expect this of Quentin or even Malik, whom Sage had referred to as a hothead, but not Dante. Sage had described him as the most mild-mannered of the bunch.

"I love Sage too much to see her hurt by someone like you."

"Someone like me?"

"Yes," Dante replied. "Don't act like you don't know. You're welcome to do as you choose with other women, but when it comes to Sage, I have to step in."

"Sage is a grown woman."

"I, along with Quentin and Malik, have looked after Sage since she was nine years old. *We,* let me correct that, *I* will not let anyone hurt her, least of all you."

"I care about Sage," Ian tried to explain. "I think she's a wonderful woman."

"That's all fine and good, but Sage wants more than an occasional roll in the hay. She may not say it, but she wants a real relationship, a commitment."

Ian was momentarily stunned. "Has she told you that?"

"She doesn't have to," Dante replied. "I know her better than she knows herself, which is why I'm here. You need to break it off."

"Excuse me?" Ian wasn't used to anyone telling him what to do. He didn't appreciate Dante coming into his office telling him how to live his life, no matter how well intentioned.

"You heard me right. You have to end this affair before Sage gets hurt further."

"I don't want Sage hurt either," Ian replied, reclining back in his chair. "I've been honest from day one and she said she was okay with the arrangement. So I see no reason to change things unless Sage tells me to do so."

Dante obviously didn't like that answer and walked toward Ian. Ian thought he was about to deck him, but instead, Dante bent down and looked him straight in the eye.

"*I'm* telling you to end this," Dante said. "Sage deserves better. She deserves to be treated with respect. She deserves to be treated like a queen by a man who loves her."

"Listen, Dante." Ian rose to his full six-foot-plus height. Usually his height intimidated most men, but Dante was not backing off. He stood prepared for battle. "I have never disrespected Sage and while she has been in my company, she has always had nothing but the best."

"I am sure you show all your lady friends the high life," Dante returned. "But Sage is not average."

Dante was certainly right about that, Ian thought. Sage was anything but average. She was smart, sexy and beautiful. She had all the qualities in a woman he was looking for if he was ready to settle down, which he wasn't. Never would be. Perhaps Dante had a point. Perhaps he should consider whether continuing a relationship was detrimental to Sage's well-being.

"Sage doesn't care about all the trappings of your wealth, Ian. She values hard work. We may have grown up poor, but Sage values people over material possessions. If she'd wanted wealth, she could have married her ex-fiancé James and had a big fancy house in Connecticut and a Mercedes-Benz in the driveway and never had to work a day in her life, but she wanted more."

"Yes, I know. She's made that perfectly clear."

"Then give her what she wants, what she deserves, or let her go."

Dante's words lingered with Ian long after he had gone. Was he being selfish wanting Sage for himself knowing that she wanted more? From the moment she'd sneaked her way into his hotel room unannounced, he'd wanted her. Desired her. He'd done everything in his power to have her, and now that he did, Ian wasn't sure he could let her go.

Sage sat at her desk and pondered whether she should go to Ian's for dinner. Her heart wanted to go full steam ahead regardless of the consequences; but another part of her, her head, told her to exercise caution. Her heart won out.

One taxi later, she was ringing the doorbell of Ian's penthouse. She was shocked when he opened the door himself.

"Hello, beautiful." Ian slid his arms around her waist and pulled her to him.

The kiss sent the pit of her stomach into a wild swirl. When he lifted his head and she caught her breath, she said, "I like the way you greet."

"C'mon inside," Ian said. He gave her a short tour of his penthouse. The penthouse, like the man himself, was nothing short of stunning. The seven-thousand-square-foot apartment had five bedrooms and six and a half baths. All the outside walls were made of glass and when Sage peered out of one, she saw a wraparound terrace. She couldn't resist walking outside. The terrace had a fabulous view of Manhattan, but the best part was a black glass mosaic infinity pool where you couldn't even see the bottom. Sage bet nearly fifty people could fit inside.

"We can skinny-dip later," Ian whispered in her ear.

"Why don't you live out in the country?" Sage asked a short while later over dinner of roast duck with blueberry sauce, mashed potatoes and grilled zucchini that his personal chef had prepared before leaving for the evening. She figured he would have a sprawling estate on the outskirts of town.

"I love Manhattan," Ian said. "Always have. I love the vibrancy, the excitement that is New York. No other city in the world has it. Not London. Paris, Rome, Moscow, Tokyo. None of them measure up." He rose from his chair and pulled Sage out of her seat. "Enough talking, I need you."

"Lead the way," Sage replied huskily.

They only made it as far as the hallway before Ian lowered his head and she stood on her tiptoes to meet his kiss. It was far from sweet; instead, it was one of mastery and possession. His lips seductively moved hers until she parted her lips and allowed his plundering tongue entry. "I missed you."

"I missed you, too," she said, reaching for him again.

They didn't make it to the bedroom. Passion carried them away somewhere between the foyer and the foot of the staircase and they began frantically pulling at each other's clothes. Neither of them seemed to care where they were. They just wanted each other right then and there.

Sage helped relieve Ian of his shirt and trousers. When she came into contact with the bulge in his shorts, she reached inside and stroked his engorged shaft. Ian groaned and his head fell to her neck. As Sage continued her ministrations, Ian lightly nipped at her neck and her earlobe with his teeth. She whipped him into a frenzy until he was moaning her name. But Ian didn't allow her to be in charge for long.

He stripped her of her jacket and camisole and when he found no bra underneath, he smiled. If he'd known that during dinner, he would have ravished her on the table. Instead, he pushed her back onto the stairs and slid her skirt and bikini panties down her toned legs.

"You are so beautiful." Ian groaned, spreading her legs and lowering his mouth to the most intimate part of her. He hovered and Sage held her breath in eager anticipation of what was sure to follow. When she felt his hot tongue at the apex of her womanhood, Sage nearly jumped off the stairs, but Ian held her in place. He tongued her with feverish delight as she writhed and moaned aloud.

"Oh, yes, Ian," Sage moaned. Her arms rested against the stairs and she threw her head back and enjoyed the thrill and feel of his hot tongue and the cold marble stair underneath her bottom. "Mmm, yes, oh, yes."

Ian loved that she was so wet and so ready for him and eager to give her all to him. "One second, baby," he said as he briefly stepped away from her to reach for his trousers. He pulled protection out of his wallet.

"And you always happen to have those around?" Sage asked.

"Hmm, if you recall, I told you anytime, anyplace," Ian said. "So I thought I had better be prepared." He slid the condom on his enlarged member and joined her back at the stairs.

He grasped her buttocks and slid inside her wet haven. He made love to her mouth as his lower body thrust against her. Her inner muscles clenched around him and Ian groaned. "Sage…" She was milking every inch of him and he couldn't get enough.

Sage clutched his buttocks as he pumped again and again. It was both heaven and hell to have Ian inside her knowing that she enjoyed their lovemaking but not knowing how long their relationship would last. The impact of that notion hit her with such force that Sage groaned and circled her arms around Ian's neck as the world became a blur.

Ian shouted several seconds later as he, too, crashed into a million pieces. When his breathing had returned, Ian withdrew and turned to sit beside her on the step.

"Wow!" Ian exclaimed as he rested his shins on the back of the stairs. "You're one hot lady." She'd surprised him with her spontaneity. He'd never expected to make love in such an unusual location. He had had his bedroom arranged for seduction with candles and soft music.

"And you're one hot guy." That was pretty evident from the trail of clothes strewn across the hallway that they had discarded in a flurry. She leaned over and kissed his cheek.

Later, they made it to his bedroom and made love again. As they lay wrapped in each other's arms, it was then that the conversation with Dante came back to haunt Ian.

Ian nuzzled Sage's forehead with his nose. "You asleep?"

"Me?" She looked up sleepily. "No."

He grinned. "Liar."

"What's up?"

Ian debated whether he should even bring it up after they'd shared such an incredible night, but he needed to know. He'd never want to hurt her; he cared about her too much. In a short time, the feisty attorney had become very important to him and he felt oddly protective.

He propped himself up on his forearm and pushed back several tendrils of damp hair out of Sage's face. "Sage, I care about you."

"I know." She smiled and caressed his cheek.

"And I would never want to do anything to hurt you," Ian finished.

"And?" Sage inquired, sitting up. Ian was beginning to make her feel very uncomfortable.

"But I need to know if you've developed feelings for me."

"What do you mean?"

"Don't play dumb, Sage. You know what I mean. Are you in love with me?"

"Why would you need to know that?" Sage countered. "Would it change anything? Would you say you loved me back?"

"As much as I don't want to lose what we have, I don't want to hurt you either."

"And I don't want to be hurt," Sage said. "So can we drop it?" She moved to turn away, but Ian halted her.

Sage knew what he needed to hear, because the alternative was much too scary for him to contemplate. Or perhaps it might snap him out of his daze and make him realize that what he wanted was staring him exactly in the face. But Sage wasn't willing to take that chance; she wasn't willing to put herself out there, so she said the words that broke her heart. "Ian, as much as I enjoy what we share, I am not in love with you."

Ian breathed a huge sigh of relief. He hadn't realized he'd been holding his breath the entire time. "Good, because I don't want to lose what we have either." He pulled her into his arms and held her to him. He wasn't quite sure he believed her, but he was too afraid to confront her because then he might have to face his own feelings and Ian wasn't ready to do that.

Sage's eyes began to water and she willed them to stop. She didn't want Ian to see that she was dying inside because of her horrible lie.

Chapter 13

"Okay, what's the deal?" Sage asked when she walked into Dante's for a relaxing evening meal with Quentin, Malik and Dante assembled. She so looked forward to the moments when it was just the four musketeers. It was already June and pretty soon Quentin would be a married man and they'd have less moments like this.

"We are worried about you," Quentin said. "Dante told us about your relationship with Ian Lawrence. So we thought we'd lend you our ears. Not to mention you missed yet another Sunday dinner. Why are you avoiding us?"

Sage narrowed her large almond-shaped eyes at Dante. She didn't appreciate being ambushed by her favorite men. She knew she'd been busy the past week now that Ian was back in town, but so what? They each had their own lives. Quentin had Avery. Malik had Peyton. And Dante had Dante's and the new restaurant.

"Don't give me that look," Dante replied. "I'm just

looking out after you, just like I have a hundred times before."

"He's right," Malik said. "We care about you, Sage, and that's why we're butting in." He gave her a devilish wink.

"Touché." Sage chuckled at her own comeuppance. Malik wasn't about to let her forget how she'd stuck her nose in his and Peyton's relationship by revealing he'd been abused by his stepfather. But if she hadn't, who knew where they would be? "This has nothing to do with Sunday dinner and everything to do with my love life." She focused her brown eyes on Dante's.

"Clearly," Malik replied. "But since when did you stop confiding in us?" Maybe Sage felt she didn't need them anymore, or that they didn't need her, which was far from the truth.

"I never stopped, Malik," Sage replied. "I guess my head is a little screwy these days."

"How can we help?" Quentin asked.

"You can't," Sage said. "I made my own bed and now I have to lie in it. I know how you all feel on the subject."

"Just because we don't approve doesn't mean you can't talk to us about it," Malik said. "We're still your family."

"I know that," Sage said. "Trust me, I do. It's the one thing I haven't forgotten, but you guys can't make someone love me. He either does or he doesn't." Her voice cracked. "And he doesn't, so I have to live with that."

"Sage, I'm sorry." Quentin wrapped his arms around her shoulders and squeezed her tightly. "I can see how much you love this guy, but if he doesn't realize what a gem he has in you, then you're well rid of him."

"Tell that to my heart." Sage sniffed.

Dante held out his handkerchief and Sage blew her

nose. She tried to hand it back, but he shook his head. "Keep it."

"So what are you going to do?"

"Ride this out until the end," Sage returned.

"You mean you're going to continue seeing him when you know he doesn't love you back?" Dante couldn't believe his ears. He just couldn't understand why Sage would subject herself to that kind of humiliation.

Sage knew it sounded ludicrous, especially when he said it like that, but Dante didn't understand the depth of her feelings. "There's a lot about Ian that you don't know or understand. He grew up like us. He understands what it's like to be alone and not have parents. And I know he cares about me. Any time with Ian is better than none at all."

"Don't tell me you're waxing poetic, that it's better to have loved and lost than never to have loved at all?" Malik didn't buy for one second that Sage was *that* sentimental.

"I've made my peace with this," Sage told her friends. "And you're just going to have to accept that."

Everything with Sage was going along swimmingly, Ian admitted to himself. Last week, Ian had cleared the air of any misconceptions she might have about their forming any commitment and now he could put Dante's warnings aside. In fact, he wanted to invite her to the breast cancer charity event he was participating in Saturday night. Although he had to be there because he'd volunteered to be auctioned off, Ian wanted Sage to bid on him so that she was the woman he went home with at the end of the evening.

Ian picked up the phone to ensure that. "Hello, gorgeous."

Sage smiled when she heard Ian's voice. "Hello, there."

"Please tell me you don't have plans for Saturday."

"Hmm, why is that?"

"Because I need you to attend this breast cancer event with me. I've been asked to participate in the bachelor auction and I want to ensure that you are the highest bidder."

"Oh, really?" she said with a smile in her voice.

"Yes, really. I'll cover whatever check you write and have the funds in your account the next morning."

"You do realize we'd be appearing in public and people might consider us an item," Sage replied.

"And I'll just comment that as my attorney, you graciously agreed to be my companion for the evening."

"I don't know." Sage was leery of going out in public with Ian. It was one thing going to his penthouse, but it was quite another going as his date to a charity event. What if it blew up in her face?

"C'mon, don't say no. I really want you there and it'll be fun."

"All right, all right." Sage chuckled at his pleading. "I'll see you Saturday."

Saturday arrived with much anticipation for Sage. She'd wanted to splurge and treat herself to a new dress at Bergdorf, but Ian had a designer one sent to her by courier earlier that morning. When she opened the box, she'd been stunned by the one-of-a-kind design. The color of cognac and made of pure silk, the gown was strapless with crinkled tiers and a mermaid skirt. She would be the belle of the ball.

"You look absolutely breathtaking," Ian said when he arrived to pick her up at her condo. He twirled her around so he could get a better look. The dress fit her like a glove, hugging her curvy bottom and petite bosom.

Sage smiled. She liked the look of appreciation in Ian's eyes. "Thank you. You look pretty good yourself." He looked masculine and powerful in his tuxedo, which she was sure cost a fortune as the cut emphasized his broad physique.

"Come here." He reached for her, but Sage stepped away.

"Uh-uh." Sage wagged her finger at him. "You'll ruin my makeup."

Ian pouted like a puppy. "You're no fun."

Sage grinned broadly. If he started kissing her, Sage doubted they'd stop and would miss the event. "Let's go."

A limousine was waiting for them outside and took them to the St. Regis hotel. A photographer snapped a shot of them exiting the vehicle. "I'm sure we'll be in the gossip rags tomorrow," Sage commented.

As they took the elevator to the penthouse, Sage thought of the explanation she would give the senior partners if they asked why she was out with a client. She would say she was his companion in the hope that she could persuade him to give the firm all of L.E.'s business.

When they exited on the roof, Ian was greeted by Lorelei Griffin, the organizer of the event. "Ian, thank you for agreeing to spotlight this event in your magazine," Lorelei said.

"No problem. It's a good cause," Ian responded and turned to Sage. "*Craze* is exclusively covering tonight's event. Lorelei, this is my attorney, Sage Anderson, with Greenberg, Hanson, Waggoner and Associates."

"It's a pleasure," Lorelei replied, extending her hand. "Welcome to the fifth annual Breast Cancer Fashion Show."

"Thank you." Sage shook the woman's hand.

"She really is quite lovely, Ian." Lorelei kissed his cheek as they entered the pavilion. "How long do you plan on keeping this one?" she murmured in his ear.

"What did she say?" Sage asked when they stepped inside.

"Just that you're beautiful," Ian whispered in her ear. He had no intention of letting Sage go anytime soon. He was having too much fun, in and out of bed. "Come, there are a few more people I want you to meet."

While he was introducing her to several influential businessmen, Sage noticed Lisa Randall, the supermodel she'd seen Ian with at the *Craze* launch party, arrive. As always, Lisa was stunningly beautiful. She was draped in a white halter dress with a black trim that just so happened to have a plunging neckline and a slit that went all the way up to her thigh. Several photographers surrounded her, eager to get the perfect shot, and Lisa ate it up.

"Everything all right?" Ian asked, smiling down at her when she'd become silent.

"I should be asking you that question." Sage inclined her head in Lisa's direction.

Ian followed her line of vision and frowned. He hoped Lisa wasn't there to start trouble. "Lisa's an ex."

"I know. She was at the launch party, remember? But she clearly doesn't want to stay that way if her presence tonight is any indication."

"Don't tell me you're jealous." Ian peered down at her. Her guard was up, so he couldn't read Sage's expression. He wondered if it had something to do with their conversation about her feelings for him.

"Not at all." Sage blinked several times and turned to face him. She wouldn't give Lisa the satisfaction. "You're here with me, aren't you?"

Ian grinned. He loved Sage's confidence. "That's right, I am." One arm circled around Sage's waist.

Sage was doing her best imitation of a stiff upper lip. She was, in fact, very unsure of their relationship. She'd given in to temptation and along the way her heart had gotten involved. Somehow, her love for Ian surpassed what she felt for Quentin, Dante or Malik, and now Ian Lawrence had his own special place there. How would he react if she expressed her true feelings? Her mind went to that afternoon aboard *Elusive* when they'd made love and Sage knew that answer. He'd run for the hills.

"We should probably get seated." With his hand on the small of her back, he led her to their table. The table for eight was nearly full when they arrived. Ian introduced her around the table and they settled in for the evening. The conversation sparkled and the dinner wasn't bad for a catered event, but it was the auction that Sage was looking forward to. Before he'd left to go backstage, Ian had told her to bid whatever it took to ensure he would end up as her date.

Lorelei was the hostess for the evening and got the auction under way. Several prestigious men she'd seen in the society pages were auctioned off for ridiculous sums of money. Sage couldn't believe how easily the wealthy threw away their money even if it was for a good cause like cancer research.

When it was Ian's turn, Sage perked up.

"Now, ladies," Lorelei began. "You all know this gentleman is one of the wealthy bachelors in town. So you know what that means…if you want a night with this guy, you're going to have to dig deep in your pockets. He is one of the most prominent men in the multimedia world today, with a media empire that spans publishing, television and radio. Ladies and gentlemen, I give you Ian Lawrence."

The curtains flew back and Ian stepped out on stage. Sage was shocked at how many women stood up clapping for him and making catcalls. She was going to have her hands full.

Ian didn't seem to mind the applause one bit. In fact, he was eating it up as he walked down the runway. He paused at the end of the runway and spun around for effect.

"The bidding is going to start at ten thousand dollars."

Sage raised her placard.

"I see ten thousand. Do I hear another bid?"

"Twelve thousand," a woman from the adjacent table offered.

"Thirteen thousand." Sage raised her placard.

"Do I hear fourteen thousand?" Lorelei asked the crowd. "Look at this man." She motioned to Ian. "He is an Adonis. Surely you can do better, ladies."

Ian helped Lorelei out by removing his tuxedo jacket, swinging it over his shoulder and spinning around. The women went wild.

"Twenty thousand," a voice from the back of the room said.

Everyone seemed shocked by the sudden jump in price and turned to find the owner of the bid. Sage's eyes landed on Lisa, standing tall and proud in the center of the room.

Sage coughed. She felt a slight strangeness in her chest but shrugged it off. She was just getting overly excited because of Lisa's shenanigans. From his stance, Sage could see that Ian was not pleased with the change of events.

"Do I hear twenty thousand, five?" Lorelei asked.

Sage raised her placard.

"Do I hear twenty-one thousand?"

"Twenty-two," Lisa threw out.

"Twenty-three thousand." There was no way Sage was

going to let Lisa get the upper hand. She fanned herself with the placard.

"Oh, it looks like we have a catfight in the works." Lorelei egged the crowd on while Ian stood uncomfortably on stage.

"Twenty-five thousand," Lisa yelled.

Sage coughed again and leaned over to grab a glass of water. She was starting to feel hot and sweaty, but she wasn't going to let the leggy model get the better of her. Sage dabbed at her brow with her napkin.

"It seems someone really wants a night with Mr. Lawrence," Lorelei told the crowd. "Who is going to challenge her?"

"Twenty-six," Sage returned.

"Thirty thousand," Lisa yelled.

Sage rose and glared at Lisa. "Thirty-five thousand."

From on stage, Ian could see the battle of the wills going on between the two women, but he knew in the end that Sage would win. He'd given her carte blanche to do whatever it took.

Lisa smiled. "Fifty thousand dollars."

Sage nearly choked and had to take a seat. She hoped another asthma attack wasn't coming on, but she was getting worried. She took several deep breaths to calm her nerves. She had never expected that Lisa wanted Ian this much. She was willing to pay anything just for an evening alone with him.

"Well, well, well…" Lorelei paused. Things were certainly getting interesting. She hadn't expected such a dramatic change of events. "Do I hear fifty-one thousand?"

Sage realized she had to go for the jugular like she did in the courtroom. No holds barred, just full-on attack. Lisa would never see this coming. This was war. Sage rose and spoke loud enough so that everyone could hear. "One hundred thousand." She turned and glared at Lisa, daring her to go higher. She hoped Ian wasn't upset; he had told her to do whatever it took to win.

The crowd went silent at the outrageous sum. "We have a bid of one hundred thousand dollars for Ian Lawrence. Any takers?" Lorelei glanced in Lisa's direction. Apparently, the amount was too high for Lisa's blood because she shook her head.

"All right, going once, going twice, *sold*." Lorelei threw down her gavel. "Mr. Lawrence is all yours at a hefty sum."

Ian quickly exited the stage to the side. Sage looked a little distressed as she made her way out of the ballroom. This was all Lisa's fault and he intended to set her straight once and for all.

Sage was nearly to the restroom when she was circumvented by Lisa in the hallway. The tall beauty stood directly in her path.

"So you think you won?" Lisa shouted at her.

"Move out of my way." Sage tried to push past her, but Lisa wouldn't budge. She was starting to have difficulty breathing and needed to use her inhaler.

"You haven't won. All you've done is make a fool of yourself. Everyone in there could see that you two are more than just attorney and client."

Ian arrived before Sage could speak. "Lisa, stop it! You're the one who is causing a scene." Several onlookers in the hallway had stopped to see what the commotion was all about. Ian came in and stood between the two women.

"Me?" Lisa laughed derisively. "Is that a joke? You're the one who is sleeping with your attorney!"

"You have gone too far." The full force of Ian's dark eyes turned on Lisa and she looked down.

Sage could hear the shocked breaths from those nearby and the thought of what this could mean to her career instantly caused her chest to tighten.

"Don't you see he's using you?" Lisa said, getting in Sage's face. "When he's done with you, he'll be on to the next woman. Hell, he was with me for six months, which was a record. Trust me when I say that Ian never stays with one woman for long. You're nothing more than a bed warmer."

When Ian turned and saw how pale and sweaty Sage was and heard her wheezing, he immediately went into alert. "Back off, Lisa!"

"What's wrong with her?" Lisa questioned. Her competition looked as if she were ready to expire.

"She has asthma." Ian circled his arm around Sage's shoulders and whispered in her ear, "Where is your inhaler?" When she didn't answer, he grabbed her purse and pulled out the inhaler. Although weak, Sage reached for it and brought it to her lips. She tried to breathe after one puff, but when her breathing still didn't returned to normal, she tried a second puff, but the inhaler went dead.

"Sage, there's no more. Do you have another?" Ian asked, searching her face.

Sage shook her head.

Before Lisa could utter another word, Ian swiftly lifted Sage into his arms and carried her down the hall to the elevator. Ian was beside himself as he waited for the elevator to descend. This was all his fault; he should have neutralized Lisa before she was allowed to run roughshod over Sage.

"Ian..." Sage eked out.

"It's okay, love. We're almost there." Ian bent down and swept his lips over her forehead.

As soon as the doors opened, Ian rushed through the lobby.

The concierge came up to him, his face etched with concern. "Sir, is she okay? Do you need any help?"

"Just get me a cab," Ian barked.

"Will do, sir." The concierge snapped his fingers and before Ian knew it, the doors opened and a taxi was in front of him. A bellman opened the taxi door and Ian slid Sage inside before jumping in himself. "Take us to the nearest hospital."

"I'm okay, really I am," Sage reassured Dante, Malik and Quentin from the emergency room hospital bed. Ian had stepped outside to make a telephone call.

"Are you sure?" Dante asked, stroking back her hair.

"I'm positive. I just got overly agitated at the bachelor auction."

"Let me look at you." Quentin looked into Sage's eyes and he didn't like what he saw. "Can you guys give me a minute?" He needed to have a one-on-one with Sage.

"We'll be outside if you need us," Malik said.

After they'd left, Quentin turned around. "So why don't you tell me what really happened." He sat down on the bed beside her and reached for her hand.

"I told you."

"You're lying. Try again." Sage wouldn't be able to lie to him when it was just the two of them. She never could. The two of them had always shared a special bond.

Sage lowered her head. She didn't like being cross-examined, least of all by Quentin. "All right, I'll tell you." She gave up. There was no way Quentin was going to take no for an answer. "Ian and I went to this bachelor auction and we ran into his not-too-distant ex-girlfriend."

"And?"

"It was awful." Just thinking about it caused Sage to reach for her oxygen mask and put it to her mouth. She breathed for a long while before venturing without it again.

Quentin waited patiently at her side. There was no way he was going to let this rest. Sage meant the world to him and he was not going to let some millionaire mistreat her, just because he thought he could.

When Sage finally found her breath, she removed her mask and continued. "She humiliated me, Quentin. After I had to outbid her for Ian by one hundred thousand dollars I might add, she confronted me in the hall and said I was having an affair with Ian. She called me a bed warmer."

Quentin punched his fist in his hand. "I could strangle that guy for putting you in this situation."

Sage threw up her hands in defense and pleaded, "Please, don't add fuel to the fire."

"So, needless to say, all of this brought on your attack?"

Sage nodded.

Quentin paced the confined area. "Ever since you met this man, you've had nothing but trouble with your asthma. He's clearly not good for you. Now you're having a secret affair with your client and his ex-girlfriend is attacking you? This is crazy, Sage. Is he really worth all this aggravation?"

Sage's eyes welled with tears. Quentin was right. She didn't even recognize herself. Her behavior of late was reckless and not like her at all. Since when did she become some sniveling, dependent freak willing to take whatever a man offered? Where was the focused, self-assured, independent woman she had always been? Where had that woman gone?

"Ah, baby, I didn't mean to make you cry." Quentin slid back beside her on the bed and wrapped his arms around her. He held her to him and lightly stroked her hair. "I just want the best for you and this guy isn't it."

"But I love him." Sage cried against his chest as she held on to him.

Quentin pulled back and looked down at her. "But does he love you?"

Sage lowered her head. That was the one question she'd avoided asking herself. "He told me he just wanted to enjoy us for as long as it lasted and I agreed."

Quentin recalled a time before Avery when he was one of those no-commitment men, but not anymore. "But somewhere along the line you fell in love with him?"

Sage nodded.

"Have you told him?"

"I can't." Sage shook her head.

"You have to, Sage," Quentin responded. "You can't continue to live a lie. If you want more, if you want a relationship, you have to tell him. You're denying what's in your heart and you're not being fair to yourself."

Sage knew what Quentin was saying was true. She'd allowed this affair with Ian to go on for too long. He was making all the rules and she was going along and it was time she put a stop to it, no matter how it might sting. Ian needed to know how she truly felt.

"Is she okay?" Jeffrey asked from the other end of the line.

"Yes, she's fine." Ian paced the sidewalk outside the E.R. "Thank God. But Lisa, on the other hand, is another matter. I need you to do two things for me, Jeffrey."

"What's that?"

"One, wire one hundred thousand dollars into Sage's checking account for the charity. And two, whatever it costs, get rid of Lisa. I don't care how much. I want her out of my life for good."

"Consider it done," Jeffrey said. "How are you?"

"I'm fine now." Ian ran his hand over his head. "It's just that…when Sage didn't respond to the inhaler…I panicked." He stepped aside when several people sought to enter the E.R. entrance.

"You care for her a great deal."

"I do."

"Perhaps you should tell her so," Jeffrey suggested. He had never seen Ian like this with any other woman. It was so clear to him how Ian felt about her, but for some reason his friend wouldn't see it. "And that's my two cents for the night. Give Sage my regards."

"I will. Oh, and Jeffrey?"

"Yes?"

"Thank you."

When he returned to the E.R., Malik and Dante stared daggers at him. "How is she?"

"Fine. No thanks to you," Dante returned and took a step toward him.

Ian didn't blame him for being upset. He should have looked after Sage better and not allowed Lisa to ambush her, but he wasn't about to let them gang up on him either.

"C'mon, Dante." Malik grabbed his arm even though he would love to take a shot at Ian. "It's not worth it and Sage certainly doesn't want you two getting into trouble."

"Fine." Dante snatched his arm and walked away down the hall. He was furious with Ian and couldn't understand how Sage would continue to allow herself to be treated this way especially by a man like him. She was usually so level-headed, so together, so sure of what she wanted.

Ian swept past them and pulled back the curtain. "How's the patient?" He smiled at Sage and then glanced at Quentin.

"I'm fine," Sage said, but then she thought about Quentin's advice. "Can you give us a minute alone?" Sage gave him a weak smile.

Quentin hated to leave her alone but he nodded. He bent down, brushed his lips across her forehead and whispered, "Just be honest." He gave Ian a withering look on his way out.

"Wow! Did it suddenly get cold in here or what?" Ian asked, rubbing his arms. It felt like the North Pole. "Because those guys—" he motioned to the curtain "—want to kill me."

"They're just worried about me," Sage said, looking up at the man she loved. "And with good reason."

"Why, is something wrong?" Ian rushed toward her, knelt down and grabbed her hand.

At the wild look in his eye, she patted his hand reassuringly. "The answer is yes. And no."

Ian's brow crinkled into a frown. "Is it your asthma?"

"No, it's not my health."

"Then what is it?"

Quentin's words came to mind again. *You have to tell him. You're denying what's in your heart and you're not being fair to yourself.*

Sage stared into Ian's eyes and wished he would declare his love for her and put her out of her misery. But he didn't, so she said, "It's us. It's this distorted relationship we're in."

Ian lowered his head. "I'm really sorry about Lisa. If I'd had any idea she was going to be there tonight I would have never invited you." He felt guilty for what happened. If it wasn't for Lisa, Sage wouldn't be in the hospital.

Sage put her fingertips to his lips. "Let me talk, please. This isn't about Lisa. This is about you and me."

"But we're doing fine, aren't we?" Ian asked. "I thought you were happy."

Sage didn't know where it came from, but somehow she summoned the courage from someplace deep and she extracted her hand from his. "No, I'm not."

"I see." Ian rose from the floor.

Sage knew he didn't want to hear what she had to say, but she had to say it. "From the get-go, I let you set the terms of our relationship. You said no commitment and I said fine."

Ian turned his back while he digested the information. "But you weren't?" He should have known. Dante had indicated that Sage wanted more, but he hadn't cared. Yet, she should have been honest with him. "So you lied?" he asked, turning around to face her.

Sage shook her head. "No. Initially, I was fine with the arrangement." When Ian looked skeptical, she repeated, "I was, but somewhere along the line, things changed for me."

"What changed?"

"I fell in love with you," Sage stated matter-of-factly and bunched her shoulders.

"Sage…" Ian tried to speak, but Sage shook her head.

"Listen, I understand you're not capable of anything more. I'm not asking you to feel something you don't feel. I know you can't make a person love you."

"I care a great deal…"

"Let me finish, please," Sage interrupted him. She needed to get the words out. "I'm not saying this to make you feel bad. I'm just letting you know that this affair or whatever it is we're doing isn't working for me anymore. That's why I'm ending it."

"You're what?" Ian stepped back. He couldn't believe his ears. Usually he was the one breaking up with someone, not the other way around. It was a little disconcerting. "I thought we enjoyed each other."

"I do enjoy you, Ian. I enjoy spending time with you and I enjoy making love with you. But plain and simple, I want more. Don't you get it? I *love* you."

Ian shook his head. "Why must women want more than I can give? Can't you see that I'm not capable of anything more?"

It broke Sage's heart to hear him toss her love aside as if it was a mere inconvenience. "If you think giving me or any woman jewels and trinkets is enough, you're wrong."

"I know I can't buy you, Sage. You've made that perfectly clear from the start," Ian said exasperatedly. "But I thought we were similar creatures that were self-sufficient and didn't need all that love stuff." Ian hung his head low and his shoulders sank. "I guess I was wrong."

"I thought we were and we do share some commonalities," Sage said. "But..."

"So you want to end this? Despite how good we are together?" He didn't want what they had to end and he stared at Sage for some sign of hope that they could continue the status quo, but there was a look of resoluteness on her face. One that signaled the end was near.

Sage wiped a tear from her eye. "I have to."

"You don't," he returned stiffly.

Sage shook her head. She had to be strong. She'd walked away from the love of her life before and she would do it again, no matter how much it hurt. "Yes, I do because if you can't give me what I want, what I need, what I deserve, then I'm going to find someone who can, someone who returns my love unconditionally."

Ian was quiet for a moment. She was right, he knew, but it still stung. He enjoyed Sage and not just her body, but also her mind and her spirit. He'd seen such a fighter in her tonight when she'd refused to let Lisa win. He'd been even more attracted to her, but lust was not enough. Sage wanted love and Ian just wasn't capable of love. He'd been without it for so long that not having it was second nature. If he cared for her, which he did, he would want her to be happy. "I understand," Ian said finally. "And although I don't *like* your decision, I will respect it."

"Thank you." Her eyes swelled when he turned to leave. "And, Ian?"

"Yes?"

"I only want the best for you." Sage wiped away the tears that were streaming down her face with the back of her hand. "And I sincerely hope that someday you will find someone you can love and who makes you truly happy."

When Ian had gone, Sage finally let out the sob that she'd been holding inside. And just like when she was a kid, Dante, Quentin and Malik rushed to her side. But this time they couldn't make it all better.

Chapter 14

"It's over between Sage and me," Ian told Jeffrey Monday morning after they had finished a board meeting at Lawrence Enterprises. Frustrated, he plopped down in his executive chair.

"Really?" Jeffrey asked. He guessed he should have known. Ian had walked into the meeting ready for bear and bitten off several executives' heads. Most had scurried out afterward, leaving Jeffrey to bear the brunt. "Did you let her down easy?"

"Actually, it was the other way around."

"Excuse me?"

"You heard right. Sage broke up with me." Ian couldn't believe he was saying the words aloud. He was still having a hard time digesting it even after restless nights spent sleeping on it. Not to mention the other body parts that craved her. All weekend, he had hoped Sage would change her mind and come back to him. She hadn't.

"Wow! How did that happen?" Jeffrey exclaimed, taking a seat opposite Ian. "Saturday night she was buying you for one hundred thousand dollars."

"Things can turn on a dime," Ian responded, snapping his fingers. "I guess she realized life was too short to stay with someone who didn't love her back."

"She told you she loved you?"

"Yes, but unlike the movies, she didn't say she couldn't live without me," Ian replied derisively. "Instead, she said she could and she would."

"Must have been a blow to your ego." Jeffrey chuckled even though he was sorry to hear it. He'd been sure that the one person who might get through to Ian, the one person he might finally open his heart to, was Sage. The poor dear had finally given up on penetrating Ian's tough exterior.

"Don't laugh at my plight." Ian rolled his eyes at Jeffrey. "I really cared for Sage."

"You just weren't ready to say that you loved her."

"Quite frankly, I doubt I could ever say those words to any woman," he confessed quietly.

"And the case?"

"Sage is a professional," Ian answered, not turning around. "I'm sure she will carry on and it will be business as usual. As if it she and I meant nothing."

Or so he hoped, thought Jeffrey.

Sage wished she had the luxury of crawling into a hole somewhere and never coming out. Her heart felt as if it was broken in two. After her breakup with James, she never thought she'd put herself out there again. But she did, just with the wrong person.

She'd known it was a mistake from the start getting involved with a man like Ian. For men like Ian, women were interchangeable. She was a fool to hope he would realize she was the right woman for him that he would let go of the past anger he had toward his father and mother and allow himself to fall in love. *She'd been wrong.* Telling him how she felt hadn't even given him a moment's pause.

Her heart was broken. She didn't force herself to put one foot in front of the other and go to work Monday. Instead, she stayed home and searched the Internet for news of the auction. She was sure someone must have heard Lisa's rant at the charity auction or that she would be on the front page of some gossip rag, but she found nothing. Not one single word was in print about her and Ian. Sage thanked her lucky stars and took it as a good sign that she'd made the right decision to end their affair before her career became collateral damage.

She used the day off to run errands and finally pick up her bridesmaid dress at the bridal boutique. She was at the checkout counter when Sage's BlackBerry vibrated. "Hello?" Patrick called to inform her that he had more incriminating information. Sage learned that Bruce Hoffman had ties to Lucas Johnson's girlfriend, Gia Smith. Gia had been working for a consulting firm for the past eight years, but had returned to the States over a year ago. She and Bruce had served on a charity committee when she was stationed at the L.A. headquarters before being sent to New York a few months ago. Gia had returned much earlier to the States than she had led Ian to believe.

"And now he just so happens to harass her boyfriend?" Sage commented. "It doesn't add up."

"It sure as hell doesn't," Patrick said from the other end.

"You've done a great job, Patrick," Sage replied. "Now I have a smoking gun." And she knew exactly what to do with it.

After she hung up, she called her assistant. "Book me a flight to Los Angeles."

"The situation with Lisa has been handled," Jeffrey told Ian in the study of his penthouse that evening.

"Thank you," Ian replied. "And I never thanked you for handling the pictures from the fashion show." Apparently, one of the *Craze* photographers had shot several pictures of the argument between Sage and Lisa. "That would have been disastrous."

"Yeah, well, it's easy when you own the only magazine covering the event," Jeffrey said, taking a seat and folding one leg across the other. "That was a pretty brilliant move on your part."

"I had no idea that would happen when I made the offer, but I'm glad I did. Because now there may be talk, but no proof."

Jeffrey smiled. "Though I must say, I'm surprised at how well you're taking the breakup."

"What did you think would happen?"

Jeffrey shrugged. "I don't know." Maybe for once, he thought Ian would allow himself to feel and see what Jeffrey already saw. He was in love with Sage.

"Nothing has changed, old boy." Ian rose and patted him on the back. "I am still the same man I always was." Even as he said the words, Ian knew he didn't mean them. In bed last night, he'd been restless. He missed having Sage. But he was who he was and he couldn't change, not even for her.

Sage smiled on her return flight from Los Angeles to New York Wednesday evening. Although it had been nothing like her first whirlwind trip, it had been very productive. The crucial person in the jigsaw puzzle of this lawsuit, Bruce Hoffman, had caved in and given up the dirt. Hoffman had not been expecting her, which was exactly what Sage had wanted because it worked to her benefit; he'd had no time to prepare.

She'd walked in confidently and informed him she knew of the ruse he, Lucas and Gia concocted to fraudulently obtain funds from Lawrence Enterprises. And if he didn't stop this nonsense immediately, he'd be up on criminal charges. For all his bluster, Bruce Hoffman had immediately spilled his guts. He'd claimed Lucas and Gia had approached him with the elaborate scheme in hope of retaliation and revenge for all the perceived wrongs against them courtesy of Ian.

Given his dislike for Ian, Bruce had jumped at the chance and agreed to publicly harass Lucas so that he'd have a legitimate racial discrimination claim, but he didn't want to go for jail for it. Instead, Bruce agreed to give up his shares of L.E. in exchange for Ian not pressing charges. Ian would finally have Bruce Hoffman out of his life and, in turn, the shares would just so happen to give him fifty-one percent of his father's company. Sage was sure once he heard the deal, Ian would agree.

Sage was giddy with excitement at her handiwork. She'd outdone herself with this one and as much as she wanted to share the information with Ian, she couldn't. Theirs was a professional relationship now and it would have to keep until normal business hours. Instead, she hopped in a taxi over to Dante's for a hot meal and a shoulder to lean on.

He wasn't there, but Quentin was. "Hey, what are you doing here all by your lonesome? And where's Dante?" she asked, walking behind the bar and storing her briefcase.

Quentin shrugged. "Don't know. He was already gone when I got here. It was kind of spur of the moment to stop by and pick up something for dinner for Avery and me. How's my girl?" Quentin pulled Sage into a big bear hug.

"I'm good." Sage disengaged herself. "I caught a break on Ian's lawsuit and should have it wrapped up in a few days."

"That's great," Quentin said. "Then you and Mr. Playboy can finally move on."

"Q…"

"Don't Q me," he replied. "I know you, Sage, and I can see that you're still in pain."

Sage's smile waned. "I guess I had forgotten how much this love stuff hurt. With James, it had been easy to throw myself into my career maybe because I didn't love him as much. But Ian, Ian snuck up on me when I wasn't looking and stole my heart."

"I know the feeling," Quentin replied. "If you remember, that's how it was with me and Avery." He thought back to over a year ago when he'd first met the love of his life. "I was a ladies' man and proud of it. But along came Avery and everything changed."

Sage remembered all too well. Quentin had been willing to toss aside a long-standing brotherhood with Malik by not publishing negative photos of Avery's biological father, Richard King, all to make Avery happy.

"That's how I feel about Ian. I wasn't looking for love. Didn't want it. Didn't need it. But when I met Ian and stopped long enough to let myself feel again, I fell hard. He made me want more. Want a future. Want an 'us.' I even wondered what it would be like to start a family with him. Can you imagine me pregnant?"

Quentin rubbed his goatee. "Actually, no."

"Hey!" Sage nudged him in the middle. "That wasn't nice."

"I was kidding." Quentin laughed. "I think you will be

a great mother one day. And you're going to make an even better godmother."

"What?" Sage stared back dumbfounded.

"Yes, Avery is pregnant, but no one knows and she would die if she knew I told you."

Sage was surprised. She couldn't imagine that the pregnancy was not planned; Avery was usually so detail-oriented.

"When did you find out?"

"A couple of days ago." Quentin beamed with pride. He'd never been happier than he was at this moment and he couldn't wait to make Avery, his baby's mother, his bride. "She's not very far along. You have to vow you won't tell a soul."

"I promise." Sage crossed her heart. "And Q?"

"Yes?"

"Thank you. You just gave me something more to smile about."

Ian was surprised when Sage walked into his office the following morning. When his assistant told him she was waiting outside, Ian felt as if his heart leaped in his chest among other body parts. He'd stalled so he could gain his composure, but as she stood in front of him in a corporate two-piece Chanel pantsuit and alligator pumps, Ian realized just how much he missed her. There were nights he'd physically ached for her, but Sage had made her intentions clear: she wanted more, more than he could offer and she wouldn't settle for anything less.

"Sage…" Ian began to rise as she walked forward.

"Don't get up." Sage motioned for him to sit down. "I have good news." She pulled a document out of her briefcase. "I have an affidavit from Bruce Hoffman stating

Lucas and Gia concocted this harassment suit so that they all could get back at you."

"So he was in cahoots with them?" Ian asked, settling back in his chair. "How did you convince one of my most-hated enemies to come clean?"

"In exchange for you not prosecuting," Sage continued, "he agreed to sell you his shares in Lawrence Enterprises."

"You're kidding." Ian jumped up out of his seat.

Sage shook her head. "It's no joke. I took the liberty of drawing up the papers to make sure they were ironclad." She pulled the document out of her file and threw it on his desk. "Signed, sealed and delivered. You now own fifty-one percent of Lawrence Enterprises."

"Sage, this is wonderful." Ian rushed toward her, lifted her off her feet and swung her around.

"Ian, put me down!" Sage laughed.

"You've no idea how happy you've made me," Ian replied. He slowly set her down on the floor, but as he did their eyes locked and it took all of Ian's strength not to kiss Sage senseless. To remind her how good they were together. How good they could be again if given the chance. *But what would that do?* They would only end up back in an untenable position. He wanted a casual relationship and she wanted a committed one.

"Ian." When Sage said his name and looked up at him with those big brown eyes, it made him want to risk it all to take her right there and love be damned. But instead, he pulled away.

"Sorry about that," he apologized.

Sage gave a weak smile. "No apologies necessary." She turned away from eyes as dark as night and inhaled. Oh, how she'd wanted him to kiss her and how good it would have felt to be in his arms again. Thankfully, he'd exercised restraint. "I've set up a meeting at my office with Lucas for later tomorrow morning. Rest assured, I will end this lawsuit."

"I have no doubt you will." Ian had never met a more determined woman.

"Okay…well…I guess…" Sage fumbled to find her words as she picked up her briefcase. "I will call you later with an update."

"I look forward to it." As Sage found her way to the elevators, she didn't see Ian standing in the doorway or the wistful look in his eyes as he watched her leave.

Chapter 15

Lucas Johnson and his attorney, Brock Campbell, walked confidently into the conference room of Greenberg, Hanson, Waggoner and Associates later the next afternoon.

"Gentlemen, please have a seat." Sage motioned to the conference table.

"I assume this meeting is because you're ready to admit defeat," Brock replied.

"Quite the contrary," Sage returned. "I'm prepared to take this to trial, a criminal trial." Sage watched as a shocked expression spread across both men's faces.

"What are you talking about, Anderson?" Brock asked.

"If this went to trial, your client would have to commit perjury." Sage narrowed her eyes on Lucas Johnson. "And therefore, the state would have grounds for a criminal trial."

Brock turned to Lucas. "What is she talking about?"

Just then, her assistant led Gia into the conference room.

When he saw her, Lucas nearly jumped out of his seat. "What are you doing here?"

"I have no idea why I'm here," Gia replied haughtily. She looked ever the sophisticated executive with her designer suit and purse tucked underneath her arm. "Would you care to explain, Ms. Anderson?" She glanced in Sage's direction. "I was summoned by *your* office."

"Of course." Sage opened up the file she'd brought with her to the conference room. "Brock, your client and his lover—" she inclined her head toward Gia "—conspired to defraud my client of millions of dollars." Sage pulled out the incriminating photos of Lucas and Gia that Patrick's firm had snapped and threw them on the table.

Brock reached for them and flipped through them. "Lucas, what is this?" He turned to his client. "Who is this woman to you and what does she have to do with this case?"

"What you have proves nothing," Lucas replied and stared coldly at Sage. "Gia and I are an item, so what?"

"He's right, plus those photos could have been doctored," Gia responded. "I've been abroad."

"No?" Sage inquired, raising a brow. She'd gotten them both unaware and knew when to go for the jugular. "How about this?" She slid a photo of Gia and Bruce Hoffman together at an L.A. charity event along with Bruce's affidavit toward Brock. "A sworn statement by your alleged harasser stating Lucas and Gia concocted this entire scheme to defraud Ian Lawrence of millions. In return for the harassment, Mr. Hoffman would receive a third of the proceeds. Now if that isn't evidence enough, I don't know what is." Sage leaned back in her chair. She smiled as Lucas and Gia's handiwork began to unravel in front of their eyes.

Brock shook his head in disbelief. "So you made this up?" He cocked his head to one side and stared at Lucas. "Did you honestly think you'd get away with it?"

"I'd like to know the answer to that question." Ian's towering presence loomed at the conference room doorway.

"As a matter of fact, I did," Lucas returned, standing up.

"Lucas!" Gia grabbed his arm. "Sit down."

"No, Gia!" Lucas snatched his arm away and strode toward Ian.

Sage wasn't sure she liked the crazy look in Lucas's eye; he looked as if he was on the verge of crossing the line. Sage reached for the phone in case she needed to dial security.

"For once, I thought I'd finally come out on top," Lucas returned. "After years of being on the bottom."

"How did you figure that?" Ian asked. He was amazed that Lucas felt he was the wronged party. He was the one being sued for millions and having his name dragged through the mud.

"I worked like a slave for your father and he returned that favor by making you CEO on his deathbed," Lucas hissed.

"I was his son," Ian stated bluntly. He stood face-to-face with Lucas and stared him dead in the eye.

"And I'd earned it."

"Like I hadn't?" Ian inquired. "Like you, I was in the trenches working my way from the bottom up. All to gain the respect of a man who barely tolerated me and only acknowledged me when it was convenient."

Sage listened and got a firsthand glimpse of what it

was like for Ian growing up with a father as cold as Myles Lawrence.

"And Gia?" Lucas replied, pulling her to her feet and circling his arm around Gia's waist. "Your father manipulated her when she was young and inexperienced."

Ian cast a glance at the woman at the center of this mess. "Gia was no ingenue and she damn well knows it."

"I know no such thing," Gia replied smoothly. "Myles Lawrence was a perverted old man who got his jollies off by having a sweet young thing at his side and I was a poor woman in need of financial assistance. Your father used me for his own gain."

"Oh, please," Ian huffed. He took a step away to gain his composure. "You knew exactly what you were doing. You saw a rich older man and jumped at the chance to snag him. Unfortunately, my father died before you could marry him and take him for all he was worth."

"You would say something so crass." Lucas snorted.

"And you're being naive. She's the manipulator." Ian pointed to Gia.

"Was I being naive when I saw you making a move on your father's girlfriend, weeks after he died?" Lucas asked, pushing Gia behind him as he faced Ian. "Your behavior was deplorable!"

"That's right." Gia pushed Lucas aside. "You remember that time, don't you, Ian?" Her voice turned soft and seductive. Sage could see just how easily she could wrap a man around her finger. "You tried to comfort me after Myles died." She laid her purse on the table and came toward him. "You acted so supportive of me and told me you would always be there for me." She laughed derisively. "What a joke that was. At the first chance, you came on to me, but I resisted your advances. That's when I slapped you and ran." She turned to Lucas. "That's when I came to your room distraught because I couldn't believe Myles's *own* son was trying to take me to bed."

Sage was surprised at what an actress Gia really was.

"Of course, *you* would have it all backward." Ian recalled the incident that Gia was mentioning, but he remembered it differently. "I invited you and Lucas for an extended stay at the mansion after my father's death because the old house was too creepy for me by myself. It was haunting living in that man's shadows, so the three of us stayed up talking and drinking half the night to help me forget. But you—" he pointed to Lucas "—couldn't stand your liquor and eventually stumbled up the stairs to bed leaving me and Gia alone. That's when Gia made her move.

"She told me it was me she'd always wanted, but I was too busy being a player and workaholic to notice her. So she hung around as my friend until my father showed an interest in her. That's when she realized it would be an opportunity to get closer to me."

"You're a liar!" Gia yelled at Ian.

"Am I?" Ian circled Gia. "I don't think so. You know what I'm saying is true." Ian searched Lucas's face for some sign that he was finally hearing the truth after all these years.

"She kissed me days after my father died. I spurned her advances. There was no way I'd sleep with a woman my father had bedded. Does any of this sound like the truth to you, Lucas?"

Lucas shook his head. "I don't believe you." He turned and walked to the window.

"Yes, you do." Ian walked over and stood behind him. "Deep down you know that Gia came on to *me*. Said she'd always wanted to be with me. But I didn't want her. I never did."

Lucas turned around to face him. "Because you had

enough women chomping at the bit to be with the rich playboy, right?" Lucas was tired of being in Ian's shadow. He didn't know how Jeffrey did it day in and day out.

"No. How could I be with a woman my father had been with?" Ian responded. "Now this lawsuit finally makes sense, Lucas. You've harbored this anger toward me for all these years. And for what? Because my father passed you over? Because of Gia and some perceived wrong against her?" Ian glanced at Gia. "Lucas, that deceitful woman isn't worth it."

"That's what you'd like me to believe."

"It's the truth."

"Well, I think you're a liar. I love Gia." Lucas walked over to Gia and clutched her arm. Sage noted that he seemed afraid to let her go because if he didn't have his anger, what would he have to hold on to? "She wouldn't lie to me."

Ian shrugged. "Believe what you will, but I know the truth and nothing happened that night between Gia and me. However, none of that matters anymore because what you both pulled is ten times worse. You tried to defraud my company and its investors of millions of dollars."

"So you're giving me the credit for this debacle." Gia laughed derisively. "Oh, please, if I were truly behind it, Ian, you would have never seen me coming."

Ian chuckled. "And you might have gotten away with it, if it hadn't been for this woman." His eyes landed on Sage's and her heart nearly stopped. He had a way of looking at her that left her breathless. "You didn't count on her."

Lucas glared at Sage. "So what now, Ian? Are you going to press charges against me?"

"No, he isn't," Gia stated matter-of-factly as she picked up her purse. "I doubt Ian wants his dirty laundry aired on the six-o'clock news."

"I could and I very well should," Ian replied. "Against you and Gia."

"Is there a 'but' in there?" Brock finally spoke. "Because although there was intent, no money has exchanged hands."

"Yes, there is a 'but,'" Ian returned. "I will not press charges against either of you. I'm tired of this whole business, but know this. In exchange I want you and your lying girlfriend out of my life and out of my business for good."

"That is very generous, Mr. Lawrence," Brock replied.

"Generous?" Lucas yelled. "He's letting us off the hook so he can blackball us." Lucas wrapped his arm around Gia.

"Blackball *you*," Gia said, extricating herself from Lucas's grasp. "*I* have a job. *I* don't work for L.E. You see, Lucas, you are and will always be a loser and I don't date losers."

"Gia, what do you mean?" Lucas asked, his voice rising slightly. "We're in this together."

"It means you and I are through," Gia replied. "This ship has sailed." Gia headed toward the door. "See you next lifetime, Ian." She inclined her head toward him and seconds later, she was gone.

"She left me." Lucas sagged into a nearby chair and shook his head. After everything he'd done to avenge her, she'd just walked out on him. "I can't believe she left me," he whispered to himself. "Are you happy now?" He glanced up and asked Ian bitterly, "Now that I have nothing?"

"Look at it this way, at least you have your freedom," Sage stated.

"There will be no blackball," Ian said. "I just want you gone."

"As you wish," Lucas said snidely. He quickly rose from his chair, turned on his heel and strode out the door.

"Sage, needless to say I had no idea they'd concocted this ruse," Brock replied.

"I know, Brock."

"No hard feelings?" He extended his hand. Gone was the bravado he'd walked in with and instead it was replaced with humbleness.

Sage smiled. "None." She shook his hand and Brock bowed on his way out of the conference room. Once they had gone, Sage spoke her mind. "I can't believe you did that. You could have easily sent Lucas and Gia to jail."

"And what purpose would that serve?" Ian asked, closing the door.

"I'm proud of you."

"Me?" Ian's voice rose. "*I* didn't do anything. It's you who should be proud. You were magnificent!"

"Magnificent. That's a bit much." Sage chuckled. "I was just doing my job."

"Was that all it was to you?" Ian asked, walking toward her, his eyes never leaving hers. "Just a job?" His large hand grasped her small one.

"Ian, don't." Sage slowly withdrew her hand, one finger at a time. She'd love nothing better than to celebrate this victory with him, but not this way. She'd gone too far to turn back now.

"Why, Sage?" Ian asked. Although her eyes were hooded underneath those gorgeous long lashes, he could still read them and he saw desire there. "I can see it in your eyes. You still want me as much as I want you."

She hated that he could see through her and still got to her. "But that's all it is for you, Ian. Sex, nothing more."

"I *care* for you deeply, Sage." *And he did.* He'd never

felt this way about any other woman before, so the fact that he cared for her and her well-being was huge.

"But not enough to make a relationship between us work?"

"I'm not capable of anything more than what I've offered," Ian responded.

"Then we have nothing left to say." Sage walked over to the table to grab her briefcase and headed for the door.

"So that's it?" Ian asked.

Sage sighed from the doorway before turning around. It broke her heart to walk away from the man she loved, but she had to for her own self-preservation. "I guess so. You'll be receiving a final invoice from G.H.W.A. for my services."

After she'd gone, Ian sat in the conference room for several long minutes. He hadn't wanted to lose Sage, but there was no other way. She wanted a man capable of love and he just wasn't that man. He couldn't love anyone or anything. His father had ensured that by taking away the only woman he'd ever loved: his mother. A woman who'd walked away from her child without a second thought and in the process damaged him forever.

"Mr. Lawrence." Peter Waggoner stopped in just as Ian was getting up to leave. "Sage told me the great news. The lawsuit has been rescinded."

"Yes." Ian nodded. "Appears it was a personal grudge."

"Well, I'm glad to see that Ms. Anderson brought it to a speedy resolution."

"She did and because of her, I've decided to give Lawrence Enterprises' business to your firm."

"That's fine news, indeed." Peter shook Ian's hand enthusiastically.

"Sage is an excellent attorney, Mr. Waggoner. I suggest

you do something about it, before another corporate mammoth takes her off your hands."

"We definitely intend to rectify that," Peter said. "I'll have the papers drawn up and sent over to you."

"Send the papers to my assistant Jeffrey and he'll take care of the details." From now on, he would let Jeffrey handle L.E. legal matters. Perhaps some distance would help him get the seductive temptress of an attorney out of his system for good.

"I did it!" Sage came bursting into Marissa's office. "I got the lawsuit against Ian Lawrence dropped."

"You did?" Marissa rose from her chair and rushed over to give Sage a congratulatory hug. "That's wonderful, Sage."

"I nailed that conniving son of a gun to the wall." Sage gleefully rubbed her hands. "He didn't know what hit him."

"Well, tell me the details." Marissa beckoned for Sage to sit down on her sofa. "How you do it?"

"I couldn't have done it without Patrick Kelly," Sage replied. "He's one of the best private investigators in the business. He followed Lucas Johnson and discovered he was having an affair with Gia Smith."

"Sounds juicy."

"It gets even better," Sage replied, taking a seat next to Marissa on the leather couch. "Apparently, Ian, Lucas and Gia were all friends and Lucas had a crush on Gia which was never returned."

"Until now."

Sage nodded. "Gia always wanted Ian and when he failed to pay her any attention, she struck up a relationship with Ian's father. When Myles Lawrence died, she thought she'd finally get her chance, but Ian rebuffed her advances."

"Leaving her a woman scorned."

"You got it!" Sage pointed to Marissa. "That's when she told Lucas that Ian seduced her and because of it, Lucas has wanted to get even with Ian ever since."

"For trying to take the woman he loved."

"Gia was overseas for years, but when she returned, they hatched this elaborate scheme and brought Bruce Hoffman into the mix. They didn't have to convince him to act as a harasser. Bruce was all too willing because he, like Lucas, had a beef with Ian over a business investment."

"Ian, I presume, is pressing charges?"

"Quite the opposite," Sage returned. "He's dropping the matter altogether, said he's tired of all the drama."

"Not many men would turn down the prospect of revenge."

"That's what makes him so unique," Sage replied.

Marissa stared at Sage and said what she'd suspected for months. "You have feelings for Ian, don't you, Sage?"

"I guess I didn't hide it very well."

"It's only obvious to those who know you."

"It doesn't matter. There's no more lawsuit, so I'm sure that's the last I'll see of Ian Lawrence."

"But that's not what you want?" Marissa pressed.

Sage shrugged. "Sometimes, you don't always get what you want in life." And this was one of those times. There was no future for her and Ian and she was just going to have to live with that. No matter how much it hurt.

"So Sage figured out that Lucas and Gia were behind this whole scam?" Jeffrey asked Ian later that evening.

Ian nodded.

"I have to admit I'm impressed," Jeffrey replied. "I thought she might get sidetracked by your personal relationship but clearly that wasn't an issue for her. Sage is a professional." Ian had made the right decision when he'd hired her firm as his corporate counsel. Not that Jeffery was shocked; Ian had been unhappy with the current counsel when they failed to end the lawsuit.

"That she is. Along with being beautiful and smart and sexy…" Ian stopped himself before he revealed too much.

Jeffrey smiled broadly. "Don't stop singing the woman's praises on my account."

"I'm not saying anything I haven't said before."

"True." It wasn't what he'd said, but how he'd said it, Jeffrey thought. Ian had it bad for Sage but refused to admit his true feelings. "So what now?"

"What do you mean?"

"The case is over. Perhaps you can see each other again and really try to make a relationship work."

"It was never really about the case and working together, though that did pose a threat," Ian said. "The issue is, Sage wants a commitment that I'm not willing to make."

"So you're willing to lose her instead? If I may be so bold, I think you're a fool, Ian. If you truly care about Sage, take the next step. Tell her she's the one."

"I can't." Ian turned away and Jeffrey could see him shutting down as he'd done hundreds of times before. Ian didn't like talking about feelings, let alone revealing his true feelings to anyone, and it was a shame because Sage was his ideal match.

Chapter 16

"We have to applaud you, Sage, on your excellent work in bringing the Lawrence lawsuit to a swift resolution," Peter Waggoner began in a special meeting with the partners on Monday morning. "You'll be receiving a special bonus."

Sage smiled. "Thank you, sir."

"Not to mention the fact that because of you we've secured one of the largest accounts we've had in a long time," Dale Hanson added.

Not just large, Sage thought to herself, a multimillion-dollar account.

"And because of your work, we'd like to extend the offer of partner to you in Greenberg, Hanson, Waggoner and Associates," Elliott said. "Which would of course facilitate a name change to Greenberg, Hanson, Waggoner, Anderson and Associates."

Sage beamed with pride. She had waited a long time

for this. From orphan to partner—she had finally arrived. "I'm honored."

"Does that mean you accept?" Elliott inquired.

"That depends," Sage replied. "What's the offer?" She'd swum with sharks the past six years and knew to look out for her best interests. She wasn't about to become the first African-American and the first woman partner at the law firm for nothing.

"Ever the attorney." Peter chuckled, but he couldn't be prouder of the work Sage had done. "It means your quarter share of the firm's profits in addition to a company vehicle, admission to our country club, a generous expense account and a hefty salary increase."

"Sounds fantastic. As long as I have the occasional weekend free, then sign me up." Although she would share in the firm's losses, she would also reap the benefits of the firm's successes.

"We're glad to have you on our team," Elliott replied and offered her his hand. "Welcome to the big league."

"Thank you, sir." Sage shook his hand.

As soon as she got back to her desk, Sage did a conference call with her three favorite men: Quentin, Dante and Malik.

"What's new, beautiful?" Malik asked. He was right in the middle of analyzing the center's expenses. "We rarely hear from you in the middle of the day."

"I have good news…" Sage paused.

"And?" the men said in unison.

"I made partner!"

"Congratulations!" Dante was the first to speak. "I knew you could do it, sweetheart."

"That's wonderful," Quentin replied from the other end. "I'm really proud of you, Sage."

Malik joined in. "Me, too, kid. You're playing with the big boys now."

"I sure am and I'm ready for it."

"We have to celebrate," Dante said. "How about a party this Saturday? You know the spot."

"I would love it!" Sage responded.

"Bring your dancing shoes," Dante replied, "Because we are going to get the party started."

Ian sat in his empty penthouse drinking scotch, reliving moments with Sage. He remembered how her face lit up when she'd seen Rodeo Drive, or when they'd ate at Il Cielo or danced underneath the stars on the beach. She'd even taken to sailing although she wasn't much good at it. None of that had mattered to Ian; he'd just wanted to be with her and he'd felt that way from the start.

He vividly remembered how she'd stared back with those dark brown eyes of hers while he stood wearing nothing but a towel and a smile. He also remembered how it had felt when he'd seen her in distress first at the penthouse and then at the fashion show. From day one, he'd felt a strong desire to protect her even though he hardly knew her.

Another part of his anatomy had taken over his brain and he'd been unable to stop himself. He'd hired her all in effort of seducing her and that he had. From the serenade, to the launch party, to Los Angeles, he'd come on full force. No holds barred and it had been well worth the wait. Sex with Sage had been incredible. Truth be told, it was the best he'd ever had. She'd been both fire and ice and it was a turn-on.

Ian swallowed another gulp of scotch. He'd heard that Sage had made partner and that Dante was throwing a party in her honor that very evening. He would love to attend to show his support and just how much he thought of her as an attorney. Of course, he hadn't been invited, but when had that ever stopped him? He didn't care how Sage's brothers felt about him. She'd been a godsend for Lawrence Enterprises. She'd saved him millions, rid him of Bruce Hoffman and gave him back controlling interest in his company. She deserved to hear it from his lips. Leaning over, he dialed his driver for a ride to Dante's.

Sage couldn't wait to party. She'd worked long and hard to make partner. As she stood at her mirror glancing at the reflection staring back at her, Sage was pleased with what she saw. She'd treated herself to a trip to the salon, so her pixie cut was freshly trimmed and stylish. Followed by a trip to Bloomingdale's for a hot new dress and some sexy stiletto sandals, a few drops of Dolce & Gabbana perfume behind each ear and pulse points, and Sage was ready to go.

She took a taxi to Dante's. She arrived fashionably late to make an entrance and found a small crowd had begun to form. Dante had really gone all-out for her. A large banner said, *Congratulations, Sage, on Making Partner,* while a large buffet table of food was lavished with all her favorite tapas: empanadas, calamari, pot stickers and beef and chicken skewers.

Marissa was there as well as Malik and Peyton, Quentin and Avery, along with a few faces from the office and a few others Sage didn't recognize.

"You know I'm so proud of you." Malik pulled her aside and kissed her cheek. "We've come a long way from our NYU days." Who would have ever thought when he and Sage had gone to college that they would become so successful? He'd received his master's in business administration while she'd gone on to law school.

"I know," Sage replied. "Who would have thought that

two orphans would end up as a big-time director over several community centers and the first black woman partner at my law firm?"

"We've achieved quite a feat, Sage. We didn't let circumstances dictate our future. We are captains of our own fate. Let's toast to our success." Malik reached over and grabbed two flutes of champagne off the bar.

"Hey, hey, hey." Dante stopped them from toasting. "None of that. You guys can't leave me and Q out. Hey, Q." He motioned for Quentin to join them. "Come over here, man. We're about to make the first toast."

"I'm coming," Quentin replied. "Excuse me, darling." He brushed his lips across Avery's. "We have to do our thing."

"I understand." Avery smiled. She didn't ever want to come between the bond he shared with his family, but she did look forward to creating their own family and they would real soon when their little boy or girl made his or her debut.

When Quentin joined the group, Dante passed a flute his way and the four of them raised their glasses. "To Sage's success." They all clicked flutes and sipped champagne.

Sage couldn't have asked for a better celebration. There was live music, courtesy of a local band that Malik knew, and great food, thanks to Dante.

"This is great," Malik commented. "And because we're all here. I'd like to announce that Peyton and I are getting hitched."

"What?" Sage couldn't believe her ears. First Quentin and now Malik was jumping the broom. What was the world coming to?

"You're kidding!" Dante exclaimed.

"No, we are very serious," Malik replied and Peyton showed off her emerald-cut diamond ring to Sage and

Avery. "It'll be a simple ceremony at the community center—not like these two." He bumped Quentin's hip.

"It shouldn't come as a shock," Peyton replied, circling her arms around Malik's waist. "You all know how much I love this man." She glanced up adoringly at him. Who would have ever thought she'd have a second chance at love?

"No, it doesn't. And we couldn't be happier for you." Sage kissed Peyton's cheek even though inside she felt a sharp pang of jealousy for what she would never have with Ian. Ian Lawrence was not the commitment kind. "Welcome to the family, although you've been one of us for a while now."

"Wow, is this orphan family expanding or what?" Quentin asked, looking around the room. A couple of years ago, it was just the four musketeers and now their family was becoming larger as they all let love in. Quentin only hoped that one day Sage and Dante would find the same kind of happiness he and Malik had discovered.

"If you'll excuse me, I'm going to go powder my nose." Sage made a hasty retreat.

She was nearly to the ladies' room when Quentin caught up with her. "Are you okay?" Sage looked distraught and ready to crumble any minute.

"No." Sage tried to hold her anguish inside, but the tears started to fall in quick succession.

"Come on." Quentin wrapped his arm around her. "Let's go outside." He led her through the double doors and into the cool night air. Once outside, Sage bent down to catch her breath.

"That's it," Quentin encouraged. "Take several deep breaths." He didn't want her having another asthma attack.

Sage took several long deep breaths and tried to collect

herself. After she could stand upright, Quentin asked, "You were so happy a moment ago, what happened?"

"This…this…" She hiccupped. "This should be the happiest time of my life… I've worked so…so hard to get here, but…"

"But something is missing," Quentin finished.

Sage nodded and wiped a stray tear from her cheek with the back of her hand. "I love him, Q, and he should be here sharing this moment with me, but he doesn't want me."

"I'm sorry, Sage. Though I know that's not what you want to hear."

"Don't, okay?" Sage raised her hand to stop him from speaking. She didn't need to hear platitudes. "You warned me and I didn't listen. You told me I was playing with fire, and I got burned." Sage paced the sidewalk. "But you know what's worst?"

"No, what's that?"

"I feel like a fool for hoping, for wishing for something more than a casual affair. There's nothing worse than loving someone who doesn't love you back."

"Come here, sweetheart." Quentin pulled Sage toward him and wrapped her in the safety of his arms. "Listen, I know it hurts now." He kissed the top of her head. "But maybe Ian Lawrence wasn't the one for you. If he didn't realize what a gem he has in you, then he's the fool. You just have to hold out for someone who really loves you."

"I hope it's before I'm old and gray." She cried into his chest.

Quentin reached out and brushed away her tears with his thumb. "You'll find love someday, Sage. Someday the right man will come along who appreciates and loves you for who you are.

"Come back inside." Quentin tugged her arm and brought her back into a room filled with people who loved her. She was thankful because it made her remember exactly how she'd gotten to where she was and she couldn't have done it without them.

When the Bentley arrived at Dante's, Ian stepped out full of fire and ready to go in and tell Sage how proud he was of her and exactly what she'd done for Lawrence Enterprises. He walked to the door ready to charge in, but no sooner than he put his hand on the handle, he got cold feet.

After the incident at the charity event, the men in Sage's family would kill him on sight and he doubted Sage wanted to see him much either. So instead of going inside, Ian stayed outside peering into the window like an outsider. He could see Sage standing in the center of the room looking as beautiful as ever. If it had been up to him, he would have continued their relationship indefinitely, but Sage wanted a commitment. Unfortunately, he'd seen years ago what loving someone could do to you. For years, he'd watched his father pine after a woman who loved someone else. Heck, more than her own son. He'd seen firsthand what love could do. How love could turn a normally sane man crazy. Love was not in the cards for him. And so, he returned to his Bentley and said, "Take me home, please."

Chapter 17

Ian's attempt to forget Sage over the past few weeks and focus his attention on his work was met with disdain by Jeffrey. He wasn't this involved in Lawrence Enterprises on a day-to-day basis; usually he left the running of his media empire to the team he'd put in place who were more than competent. They were the cream of the crop. This time was different. For the first time, he couldn't shake a woman out of his mind. Of course, Sage wasn't just any woman, which was why he was driving his staff crazy.

He'd asked for advertising sales figures for several of his television stations, examined every number much to his sales force's chagrin, reworked *Craze*'s magazine cover and ripped a young writer's article to shreds, sending her crying from the editorial meeting. He was on a tear and anyone in his path shook in fear. Ian supposed that was why Jeffrey arranged a few choice appearances at the latest restaurants and hot spots to get his attention on something else and off everyone's back.

Ian had agreed, against his better judgment, to a date with Jade Reynolds, an upcoming young actress on a new television drama. She was beautiful enough, but something was missing. He'd thought he could go back to the way he was before, moving from one woman to the next, but instead, all he could think about was Sage.

He ended the evening early and escorted Jade back to her apartment. "I'm sorry, Jade," Ian apologized as he walked her to her door and held out his hand for a handshake.

"I have to admit I'm surprised you're turning down a night in my bed," Jade replied with her hands on her hips. "Everyone told me you were a man who loved women. This is a real disappointment."

He nodded. "And they were right, I did."

"*Did,* meaning past tense? What's the problem, Ian?"

Ian paused and for once answered the question truthfully. "The problem is…I want only one woman."

Jade chuckled. "So someone has managed to tame the great Ian Lawrence, playboy to the stars. Wow! I'm impressed. She's one lucky woman."

"No," Ian returned. "I'm a lucky man."

As he drove away from Jade's condominium, Ian realized what he'd known for a long time but refused to admit. He was in love with Sage Anderson, but he'd walked away from the love. Why? Because he was afraid to love anyone, he admitted to himself.

Sage had changed that. She'd given herself over to him and what had he done with her love? He'd thrown it back in her face as if it meant nothing. The question was, would she take him back now that he was ready to love? Would she give him another chance to make it right?

* * *

"Can you believe Quentin and Avery's wedding is tomorrow?" Sage asked Dante on the cab ride over to the happy couple's rehearsal dinner at one of their favorite restaurants in Manhattan. "Time really flew." With moving into her new office and her new assignments, Sage had hardly had a chance to breathe, let alone think about a certain publishing magnate with bedroom eyes and a killer physique. Her focus had been the bride-to-be and the big event. It had to be. Yet something was missing. Her breakup with Ian had forced Sage to take a long hard look at her life. She finally had everything she wanted. She'd made partner at Greenberg, Hanson, Waggoner and now Anderson and Associates, but she wanted more.

Case in point, Ian had already gone back to his playboy ways. Sage had picked up a tabloid just the other day and seen him splashed over the headlines. Same ol' Ian.

"I know," Dante replied. "And I still have to come up with my toast for the reception." He and Malik were both best men and Malik already knew what he was going to say.

"You'll think of something." Sage smiled. "I've never known you to be at a loss for words."

"It's good to see you smiling again." Dante glanced over in her direction. Over the past few weeks, she'd looked pretty miserable despite having achieved her long-held dream of making partner. He knew she was still struggling with her feelings for Lawrence.

Sage gave Dante a tentative smile. "I've just been taking it one day at time and sometimes it's hard knowing that Ian doesn't want or return my love. But I'm trying to make peace with it."

"I'm not surprised. You've always been a tough cookie," Dante said, lightly stroking her cheek. "How else to explain how you've dealt with three male egos for the past twenty years?"

"Hmm…" Sage rubbed her chin. "You have a point there."

Once they arrived, the host ushered them into a beautifully decorated banquet room filled with several long tables. Veronica and Clay Roberts, Avery's parents, were center stage standing by their daughter, but Quentin didn't have any family standing by his side, until now.

"Q." Sage came forward and tucked her arm inside his. "We're here."

"Thank you." Quentin sighed loudly. He was relieved to see their smiling faces. "I hadn't realized just how alone I felt until Avery's relatives started pouring in."

"Well, you're not alone anymore, man." Dante gave him a pat on the back. "Your family is here."

A half hour later, Malik and Peyton arrived. "Sorry, I'm late, Q. I had a fire to put out at the Harlem Community Center."

"No worries. Just join these two knuckleheads at my side." Quentin laughed.

"Hey!" Sage nudged Quentin in the middle. "No name-calling or I'm going to leave you here by yourself," she teased.

"Congrats, Q." Peyton leaned in and kissed Quentin's cheek before taking a seat at Quentin's "family" table. Despite his soon-to-be mother-in-law's desire that they mingle, Quentin had insisted that they all sit together.

"I'm really glad to have you all here," Quentin whispered. "Because I'm nervous as all hell about tomorrow." He knew he loved Avery with all his heart, but saying "I do" in front of a crowd of folks was nerve-wracking to say the least. He guessed the guest count was upward of two hundred.

"Don't be," Malik said. "You're marrying the woman of

your dreams. What could be better than that?" He couldn't wait to make an honest woman out of Peyton.

"Not a thing." Quentin grinned. "Not a thing."

"I've made a real mess of things, haven't I?" Ian commented. He'd asked Jeffrey to meet him at his penthouse for a stiff drink after work and revealed his true feelings for Sage, which was that he was head over heels for her. He'd called Sage's office earlier and had been told that she'd left early for the day. He'd charmed her assistant into revealing that she would be attending Quentin's wedding rehearsal dinner. Now he just had to figure out what to do.

Jeffrey didn't sugarcoat his response. "I'm not going to lie to you, Ian. You're in the doghouse. You reeled the woman in and when you finally had her, you tossed her back into the ocean."

Ian glared at Jeffrey. "I wasn't that bad, was I?"

Jeffrey glared at him.

"Okay, I suppose I was. So how do I get her back?" Ian asked his most trusted advisor and best friend. This was all new to him. He wasn't used to putting himself out there. What if she rejected his love just as he'd rejected hers?

"Be honest," Jeffrey stated. "Tell her she's the only woman for you and *beg* her to take you back."

The bartender slid Ian a scotch on the rocks and Jeffrey a whiskey. Ian took a generous sip, even though he knew liquid courage would do him little good. "You make it sound so easy, Jeffrey. But you know I have never been someone to express my emotions freely."

He was right. Ian rarely expressed his true emotions except when his father died. Jeffrey swore he'd seen a stray tear at the cemetery when they'd laid Myles Lawrence to rest. But no sooner than he saw it, Ian had been back to being stalwart. "Well, you're going to have to lay your heart on the line if you want Sage back," he responded. "There's no easy way around this, Ian. You're going to have to say the three words you've been dreading to say your entire life."

"What if I tell her I love her and she still doesn't take me back?" Ian asked. He was used to getting what he wanted and he wanted Sage badly and not just for his bed partner, but for a lifetime.

"That's a risk you're going to have to take, my friend."

Ian thought about what Jeffrey said and knew he was right. It was amazing how he could take a risk on a business investment or on real estate, yet when it came to matters of the heart, to love, he found himself running scared. He'd been a coward and let the best thing that had happened to him go. When she'd told him she'd loved him, he should have embraced her with open arms. Now if there was any chance he could salvage what they'd shared, he was going to have to be open with Sage and pray that she could see he was sincere and head over heels for her.

Sage heard everyone discussing how delicious the food at the rehearsal dinner was, but she'd only taken a few bites and shuffled the rest of the chicken cordon bleu, mashed potatoes and asparagus from one side of the plate to the other.

As she watched Quentin and Avery bask in love's glow, Sage had to admit that although she was happy for him, she was a little envious of what they shared. She was also coming to accept that she and Ian would never be.

It was a cold realization, but she had to face facts. He was commitment-phobic, easily content with the status quo. Loving her would complicate his life and that, Ian Lawrence would never have. He would never give up control of his heart without knowing it was a sure thing.

And in love, no one could ever be certain. You had to take risks and believe that the love you have for the other person can withstand the storm. That was what Quentin and Avery would be doing tomorrow, taking that leap of faith.

While she wallowed in what would never be, Quentin and Avery rose to give a few short speeches. Avery thanked her parents and her best friend, Jenna, for help with the wedding and bridal shower.

Quentin was last to raise his flute. "As most of you saw, I don't have a mother or father here with me today. But who I do have are my friends…no, correction, my sister and brothers, Sage, Dante and Malik." He turned to face them. "We've weathered some rough times together, shared some highs and some lows, but despite it all, you are the best family I…" Quentin choked a little on his words. "I could ever have."

Tears welled in Sage's eyes at his warm words.

"I want to thank you for supporting me, encouraging me, loving me all these years and although I move into a different phase of my life and join Avery into our tight-knit family, you guys will always be with me and will forever be my family."

"Oh, man." Dante sighed from Sage's side as his eyes teared up. "Is he trying to make a grown man cry?" Dante reached for his water glass.

"I'm close to crying, man, real close," Malik whispered from his other side as Peyton patted his knee.

"If you guys will excuse me for a minute." Sage rose from the table and headed toward the restroom. She hadn't realized tears were streaming down her face until she felt her face become damp. She needed time to compose herself before going back in.

Thankfully, the women's room was empty. Sage glanced at her reflection in the mirror and noted her red eyes. Was she crying because of Q's speech or because she feared she'd never have a love like Quentin and Avery's?

"Excuse me, I'm here for the Davis-Roberts rehearsal dinner," Ian told the host when he arrived to the restaurant where the rehearsal dinner was being held.

The host glanced down at his watch. "Sir, the party is already under way and you've missed dinner." A tone of disdain was in the host's voice at the interruption.

"I realize that," Ian replied curtly. "But I really need to see one of the guests at the dinner."

"So be it. It's down the hall and to the left." The host waved his hand to the left.

"Thank you." Ian rushed down the hall. He didn't know what he was going to say when he saw Sage, but somehow he would find the words to tell her just how much she meant to him and that he couldn't see his life without her in it.

Ian found the correct banquet room down the hall. It read: Davis-Roberts Wedding Rehearsal Dinner. Ian pulled opened the French double doors and glanced among the crowd. He saw Quentin and Avery at the head of the room, but no Sage. He finally laid eyes on Dante and Malik at a table nearby, but still no Sage. He knew neither of the gentlemen would be too happy to see him. He'd hurt their sister, so they would be in full protective mode right now and he would expect nothing less. But Ian wasn't giving up; he was there for Sage and he wasn't leaving without her.

Determined, he walked through the crowd until he arrived at their table. Dante was the first to look up and when he did, a pair of stormy brown eyes connected with Ian's dark ones, but Ian would not be put off.

Dante immediately rose and nudged Malik. Once again, Ian received another withering look.

If You So Desire

Ian held up his hands in defense from the onslaught he knew was to follow. "Listen, I know you guys don't want me here, but I'm not leaving until I see Sage."

"Oh, you're leaving," Malik returned, punching his fists in his hand as he stood up. "One way or another."

"Malik!" Peyton jumped up out of her chair and grabbed his arm. She loved her man, but he did have a quick temper.

"Peyton, this guy used Sage and when he was done with her, he tossed her aside." Malik took a threatening step toward Ian. "And I for one am not about to let him get away with it."

"I agree. There's nothing I'd like better than to rearrange his face," Dante added.

Oh, great. Ian sighed and looked upward. He didn't want to fight Sage's family. It certainly wouldn't win him any brownie points with the lady, but he would if he had to. He glanced across the room and saw Quentin look his way. Ian didn't want to spoil his night either. Luckily, he didn't have to because a feminine voice behind him spat out, "What the hell are you doing here?"

When he turned around, Ian was happy to see Sage. She looked stunning in a one-shoulder bubble dress that hit just above her knee, revealing her beautiful brown legs. The fuchsia color was bold, beautiful and bright just like the lady herself.

"I'm here, Ian." Sage put up her first two fingers and motioned to her face when she caught him eyeing her up and down.

Ian blinked several times to snap himself out of his daze. "I know and I'm happy to see you."

"Is that a fact?" Sage couldn't believe he was standing in front of her. She hadn't heard from him in over a month. *Why had he come?* She was making her peace with how they'd ended things. Why did he have to come back now?

"Can we talk privately?" He'd prefer to say what he had to say with just the two of them present.

"Why?" Sage asked, folding her arms across her chest. "It must be important if you're here. So spit it out." She glanced in Quentin and Avery's direction and mouthed, "I'm sorry." She wasn't trying to spoil their evening, but neither was she going to let Ian sneak his way back into her heart. She needed backup, which Malik and Dante would provide.

Ian swallowed as several sets of eyes shot daggers at him.

"Speak."

"Sage, if you want us to handle this guy for you, we can." Malik spoke up.

"No, he came here to say something," Sage responded, glaring at Ian. "And I want to hear it. So speak."

"Okay…" Ian glanced around the room. The entire group was looking and waiting on him. He hadn't intended to lay his heart on the line with an audience listening. "Well, if this is how it has to be, then here goes," he replied. "You were right about me, I'm a playboy."

"See, I told you so." Malik took a step forward.

But Ian held up his hand to fend him off. "Or at least you *were*. I was a playboy and proud of it. I was used to having anything and anyone I wanted, and from the moment you sneaked into my hotel room, I knew I had to have you."

"You're not telling me something I don't already know," Sage said. Although she wasn't entirely blameless, he had been relentless in his pursuit of her.

"I stopped at nothing to have you. I used every excuse in the book and I manipulated the situation to suit my own needs."

"Go on."

"I even chose your firm for the lawsuit because I was attracted to you. But somewhere along the line, Sage, something changed for me. I don't know when exactly it happened, maybe it was that day aboard my boat, but somewhere along the line I fell in love with you."

A silence fell over the table and even Sage was taken aback. *Did he just say he loved her?* Those were certainly not the words she expected to hear. When she'd seen Ian, she thought he was coming back to stake his claim, as if he had a right to her. As if she was his possession. But love? *Love?* She hadn't expected to hear those words.

"I refused to admit it to you, let alone myself. I hid behind my reputation and my past. A past I've allowed to define me for too darn long. I've let what my father said define me and become a self-fulfilling prophecy. He told me love made people blind. I saw my mother leave my father for another man. I saw her abandon her child for a man. So the more he said it, the more I believed it."

"I don't understand."

"Don't you see? I thought that love was synonymous with hurt. I saw how my father became bitter when love turned sour on him and I never wanted to end up like him. So I closed myself off to love."

"I know because when you felt us getting closer, despite how intimate we were, I could see you drifting further and further away from me," Sage responded. "And that hurt. It's why I ended things between us."

"And trust me when I say this, I didn't want to let you go," Ian responded. "That night in the hospital broke my heart and again when you figured out what that bastard Lucas Johnson was up to. I tried to express how I felt then, that I didn't want to lose you, but I couldn't. I was denying my feelings for you, Sage. That's why I tried to go back to my old ways, but I couldn't."

"You couldn't?" She'd thought he was off gallivanting with every woman in New York. She'd been sure of it.

"I couldn't think about being with another woman because the only woman I wanted was *you*." He grabbed her hand and tried to pull her toward him, but she turned away.

Everything he was saying was what she wanted to hear, but could she believe him? "I don't know…"

"I love you, Sage, and I know I've hurt you, but I'm asking you, begging you, to give me another chance. Let me make this right, baby." He bent down on one knee. "Please give me another chance."

When Sage turned back around, her eyes were misted with tears. "I want to believe you, but maybe you were right. Maybe you're just not capable of loving another person, of opening yourself up completely." She understood being damaged goods because she'd thought she was after her mother abandoned her, but she wasn't. She was a strong, independent woman capable of loving.

"Baby, I'm here right now in a room full of people." Ian glanced around because the room had suddenly become quiet as everyone listened to their conversation. Even Dante and Malik had backed away and sat down. "Professing my love to you. It doesn't get any more open than this."

"I admit this is a grand romantic gesture," Sage said, motioning to the crowd. "But what about those quiet moments when it's just the two of us? Will you love me then? Will you stay then?"

"Give me a chance to prove it to you." Ian looked up at Sage. He could see she was waffling. "And you'll see that you're wrong. I promise I will never leave you again."

Sage paused. She knew in her heart what the answer

was, but she couldn't verbalize it. She nodded instead and Ian rose and swept her off her feet in front of the entire crowd, crushing his lips to hers in a frenzied kiss that left her breathless.

"Just know this," she said as he finally lowered her to the floor among cheers and catcalls in the dining hall. "You have your work cut out for you."

"I know." Ian grinned. "And I look forward to showing you tonight—" he bent his head so only she could hear "—in bed."

* * * * *

LVE IN THE LIMELIGHT
Fantasy, Fame and Fortune...Hollywood-Style!

Book #1

By *New York Times* and *USA TODAY*
Bestselling Author Brenda Jackson

STAR OF HIS HEART
August 2010

Book #2

By A.C. Arthur

SING YOUR PLEASURE
September 2010

Book #3

By Ann Christopher

SEDUCED ON THE RED CARPET
October 2010

Book #4

By *Essence* Bestselling Author Adrianne Byrd

LOVERS PREMIERE
November 2010

Set in Hollywood's entertainment industry,
two unstoppable sisters and their two friends
find romance, glamour and dreams-come-true.

REQUEST YOUR FREE BOOKS!

2 FREE NOVELS
PLUS 2 FREE GIFTS!

KIMANI™
ROMANCE

Love's ultimate destination!

YES! Please send me 2 FREE Kimani™ Romance novels and my 2 FREE gifts (gifts are worth about $10). After receiving them, if I don't wish to receive any more books, I can return the shipping statement marked "cancel." If I don't cancel, I will receive 4 brand-new novels every month and be billed just $4.69 per book in the U.S. or $5.24 per book in Canada. That's a saving of over 20% off the cover price. It's quite a bargain! Shipping and handling is just 50¢ per book.* I understand that accepting the 2 free books and gifts places me under no obligation to buy anything. I can always return a shipment and cancel at any time. Even if I never buy another book from Kimani Press, the two free books and gifts are mine to keep forever.

168/368 XDN E7PZ

Name	(PLEASE PRINT)

Address		Apt. #

City	State/Prov.	Zip/Postal Code

Signature (if under 18, a parent or guardian must sign)

Mail to **The Reader Service:**

IN U.S.A.: P.O. Box 1867, Buffalo, NY 14240-1867
IN CANADA: P.O. Box 609, Fort Erie, Ontario L2A 5X3

Not valid for current subscribers to Kimani Romance books.

Want to try two free books from another line?
Call 1-800-873-8635 or visit www.morefreebooks.com.

* Terms and prices subject to change without notice. Prices do not include applicable taxes. N.Y. residents add applicable sales tax. Canadian residents will be charged applicable provincial taxes and GST. Offer not valid in Quebec. This offer is limited to one order per household. All orders subject to approval. Credit or debit balances in a customer's account(s) may be offset by any other outstanding balance owed by or to the customer. Please allow 4 to 6 weeks for delivery. Offer available while quantities last.

Your Privacy: Kimani Press is committed to protecting your privacy. Our Privacy Policy is available online at www.eHarlequin.com or upon request from the Reader Service. From time to time we make our lists of customers available to reputable third parties who may have a product or service of interest to you. If you would prefer we not share your name and address, please check here. ☐

Help us get it right—We strive for accurate, respectful and relevant communications. To clarify or modify your communication preferences, visit us at www.ReaderService.com/consumerschoice.

KROM10R

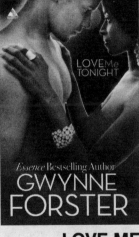